GROOM GAMBLE

EVIE ROSE

Copyright © 2024 by Evie Rose

All rights reserved.

No part of this book may be reproduced in any form or by any electronic or mechanical means, including information storage and retrieval systems, without written permission from the author, except for the use of brief quotations in a book review.

This story is a work of fiction. Names, characters, places, and incidents are the product of the author's imagination or are used fictitiously. Any resemblance to actual events, locales, or persons, living or dead, is coincidental.

Cover: © 2024 by Angela Haddon.

❀ Created with Vellum

1

SOPHIA

I'm making a list of requirements for a husband. I know this isn't usually how marriage works, but I'm a bit desperate.

So far, I have:

- Tall. Over 6 foot 3.
- Black hair. Touch of silver at the temples would be a bonus.
- 40+ years old.
- Nice smile.
- Short beard.
- Grey eyes.

The level of delusion here is quite impressive. Twenty-three years old, and I am resorting to an arranged marriage, but I'll marry anyone who meets these criteria, because I'm describing *my boss*.

Sigh.

It's ridiculous, really, using a matchmaker. I'm a solid six out of ten, and my sense of humour is at least a six-point-five. I saw Mr Streatham hide a quirk at the corner of his mouth when I called my new filing system "witness protection for documents". I have a degree in Business Studies, and an intact V-card. I have a job that's amazingly paid, even if I only get the absolute minimum holiday. I swear, if my boss made me work any more we'd both have to sleep at the office.

The problem is, I'm shy. I prefer books and dogs to parties and people.

Although, I made an exception for Mr Streatham, six months ago. He is the one person I like.

His previous assistant warned me I probably wouldn't. She said he was abrasive, and difficult, would occasionally arrive back in the office after a murder, but be fair and try not to drip blood on the carpet. He expects total commitment.

And it's reasonable. He's perfect, and demands perfection. He likes tradition. Paper, ink, handwritten or printed in a newspaper-style font. Mr Streatham prefers things to be in his hands, not in pixels.

My boss might be a growly, grumpy mafia boss who murders anyone who gets in his way, but with me he's got classic chivalry. He's never so much as touched a hair on my head. No inappropriate looks. No brushing up against me in the corridor. He holds doors for me and while he barks orders, he's so careful. Never crass. Mr Streatham is like a sexy professor, but with an edge of danger.

I adore him, old-school ways and all. And I love that he relies on me, his assistant.

I wish he'd lose that cool and take my virginity over his desk.

Sometimes, when I'm lying in my bed at night, and I can't sleep for longing to be back at work and have Mr Streatham rumble, "Good girl" and give me a slight smile when I've pleased him, I reach between my legs and imagine what it would be like to have my boss' weight on top of me. What he'd feel like inside me.

And I will never know that, because I am going to get married to a stranger who probably has a boring job, medium height, unremarkable eyes, a sensible tolerance for failure, and a desire for children.

I add "rich" to the list, because if I'm putting Mr Streatham's physical details in here, I might as well go all the way.

- Likes me.
- Good hygiene.

I cross that out and write *perfect* hygiene. Because my boss always smells amazing. Like black pepper and cardamom with an undertone of smoky leather. And if I have to compromise and not have a nosegasm, I at least don't want BO.

It's weird, but I think better on paper these days. I used to make notes on my phone or a computer, but since working for Mr Streatham, I've picked up on his paper addiction. He loves books as much as I do, and his office is lined with special editions of the crime novels he likes, and non-fiction books, mainly about murders and spies. I'd find it creepy, but he's a mafia boss. I guess it's like market research.

I add to my list.

- Educated.
- Loves books.

Then I think for a moment. Perhaps I'll edit this before

I send it to *London MatchMakers*. I'll need to type it up into an email anyway. This could be a fantasy list of my ideal husband, and I'll reduce it to something realistic afterwards. But given I'm going to compromise on my choice of life partner, perhaps I should allow myself to dream?

- Powerful.
- Kind.

You wouldn't think a mafia boss would be kind, but Mr Streatham is good to me, in his own gruff way. He's a member of the London Mafia Syndicate too, and the rumour is that they are behind some of the changes for the better in London. And he always pauses to stroke the stray cat that likes to hang out in the entrance hall.

- Good with animals.
- Good with children.

Honestly though, I'm dancing around the point here: the whole reason for getting married rather than just adopting a few cats and crushing on my boss for the rest of my life.

- Wants children. At least five.

Maybe that's excessive, but this whole impulse was triggered when I was researching the Essex Cartel for a report, and then started reading about the London mafia bosses and their marriages. The Fulham kingpin and his wife are on record saying they're aiming for ten kids. I turned so green with envy you could have stacked me in the vegetable aisle, and someone would have put me in their shopping basket thinking I was a broccoli.

But if I want that many kids, I gotta get started. Which means finding a husband. Pronto.

I check my watch—another thing I've changed since working for Mr Streatham. I used to use my phone, but I enjoy the elegance and simplicity of the little round face on a dainty strap around my wrist. I feel like a girl in an old movie. Five minutes until the end of my lunch break. Mr Streatham will be back soon. Anticipation and adrenaline pulse from my chest, all down my arms and I scrawl two more requirements at the bottom of the list, then look at the top items again, as though by ignoring those items I can deny that I'm such a slut that I could even think that, never mind write it down.

But honestly, if I want a baby, I should ensure my husband is up to the job, right? Maybe I'll ask for a fertility test. There are discreet home kits. Probably.

I'm not being unreasonable.

There are quick steps in the corridor and my brain freezes. What, no, oh, gah. It's okay, it'll just be someone from HR or—the door opens and Mr Streatham strides in, a determined glint in his eye.

I shove my list into the out tray and pin a sunny smile on my face.

"There's a fuck-up with Operation Calculus, Miss Berry, and you need to fix it," he says without preamble.

Snatching up a sheet of paper, I scribble down the details as he stands before me, a shadowed mountain, one hand massaging his forehead. He rattles off payments to be made to the various Essex Cartel men he's bribing for information, and how it is to be delivered. A mix of crypto, purchases to their legitimate businesses, and good old-fashioned cash. It still has a place in the mafia, if not the rest of the world.

"Or should I just have them killed, and not risk it?" he finishes. "No, scrap that, make hit notes for—"

"Better to have a live asset than a dead liability," I chirp. Those are his words. A Streatham motto, as it were.

"Mmmm." He nods grimly, looks up, then stills.

His sharp gaze recognises something is off, despite my efforts. He scans my face, then my workspace, and presumably finds nothing amiss until he focuses on my watch. "Add five minutes onto your bonus request for this month, please, and label it, 'The Essex Cartel screwed up our lunch break'."

I write it into my agenda, hand shaking, telling myself this is going to be okay. No one will die today, of mortification or any other cause. Probably.

Mr Streatham gives a weary sigh and heads to his office, and I ease out a breath.

It's fine. It's all fine.

"The virginity thing." He turns back.

"What?" I squeak. How can he know?! I check myself, as though maybe I have it written on my top. Nope, nope, it's okay. A person still doesn't have their sexual status emblazoned across their chest. *Calm, Sophia.*

Besides, if Mr Streatham could tell, it would be an alpha-male pheromone thing, right? He's so big and masculine, he could have wolf-shifter senses.

"The paperwork on it." Mr Streatham frowns at my weird reaction.

Paper. My mind springs to my list.

Oh nooooo. He must have seen it somehow.

"I don't know what you're talking about," I say, trying to sound innocent.

Mr Streatham gives an impatient growl and shakes his head. "That Essex Cartel auction nonsense. Did you finish it, or not?"

A report. On the virginity auctions that the Essex Cartel runs.

Yes. Obviously. He had me compile a report, with a focus on whether the young women consented to taking part.

"Yes!" It comes out a bit over-enthusiastic, because the relief is palpable. My boss remains ignorant that his assistant is a sad virgin girl with a crush on him. Phew.

The whole report may have made me inconveniently horny, and been part of why I am now intending to get married. Because as scandalous and awful and morally bankrupt as the auctions and public sex are, they're also… Kind of hot?

"Could I have the report, please?" he asks, with a twist of sarcasm when I just stand there, unmoving. "Or is it too naughty for a London Mafia Boss?"

"Yes," I say hurriedly, trying to remember where it is. I dive forwards and scrabble around in my files.

"It *is* too naughty," he drawls. "So you've hidden it."

"No!" Paper flies everywhere as I try to find the report. Printed out, of course. "I could swear it was…" Somewhere? Admittedly, I was rather focused on my list this morning, so my flustered little brain has forgotten where I filed it. There are dozens of letters and reports all stacked, it must be there.

"I'll bring it through!" I say brightly, popping my head up.

Mr Streatham's gaze flicks to my face, as though he was looking elsewhere. He folds his arms and narrows his eyes, confused. And no wonder. I don't usually keep him waiting for anything. I never lose things.

"I can wait." His voice and stance announce he will resent every moment I delay him.

My cheeks pinken and I try to regulate my breathing as I flick through more documents under his cool silver regard. "I'm sure it's... Ah!"

The right report!

At the bottom of the out tray. Who knows why it was there? I drag out the little stack of sheets secured with a paperclip, and thrust them at my boss.

Mr Streatham's steel eyes have a question in them as he accepts the report, but with only a slight hesitation and lowering of his brows, he turns away.

When the catch snicks closed on my boss' office door, I sag with relief.

Now, I just need to put that humiliating list in my purse and continue with a normal day.

2

DEX

Sometimes, I wish I was not a morally grey London mafia boss.

I stare at the door that separates me from my little assistant.

For Sophia—Miss Berry, even her name is cute—I wish I was a man worthy of her. I wish I were whatever she wanted.

But no. I continue to be a grumpy kingpin too old and too much her employer for the depraved ideas that go through my head when I see the smallest peek of her breasts as she leans forward.

I am an arsehole. I should put Miss Berry well out of harm's way, so I'm not tempted to pluck her and suck on her sweet juices.

I toss the report onto my desk and go to the window, which overlooks the large green space of Streatham Common, the formal garden close to the office leading to fields and woods beyond. It's a little oasis in the hubbub of London, and I've loved it since I was a kid in this building helping my dad. I'm not sure when it became so painful to look. The sight of families used to soothe me, an indication of the peace and prosperity Streatham represents, even if it's underpinned by violence to keep order.

Now, it just reminds me how alone I am, up in this towering old mansion.

Fucking hell. What's the matter with me?

I grind my teeth, because I know what's wrong. It's the distance between my adorable assistant next door, and me in this creaky office.

Yes, the work on infiltrating the Essex Cartel and removing the less desirable parts is important. Those pricks are far too comfortable, and need to be brought in line. The coup I'm arranging on behalf of the London Mafia Syndicate will achieve that, but I'm not personally invested in it. I have no wife or children to give my life meaning, I'm in effortless control of the London territory that has been in my family for four generations. The coup engages me on an intellectual level, not emotional.

None of that was a problem until six months ago when my executive assistant retired—much against my wishes but I suppose she had a right at seventy-five—and hand-selected her replacement. I walked into my office and had my heart ripped out by a sweet and sunny girl who glanced at me from under her lashes and nervously fiddled with her hair.

Too young. Too innocent. Too good.

So breedable.

Twenty-three years old to my almost forty, and practically gifted to me by her predecessor, who I swear smirked before she said "goodbye" and that she was certain we'd "get on well".

There was always something about Miss Berry, from the first day when my fingers constantly itched to tuck that strand of caramel and chocolate hair behind her ear. She's competent, and cheerful and sweet, yes. But she's also gorgeous.

She makes it hard for me to think. Or she just makes me hard.

I consider a furtive wank to take the edge off. That skirt Miss Berry is wearing today? Ooof. Made for sin. But I know from experience that will leave me feeling even more hollow, and much as the fantasy that she'd walk in on me and offer to help is hot as fuck, I have spent six months pretending I'm a man with morals, and best not to give up now.

Instead, I sit down and flick through the report on the Essex Cartel's barbaric virginity auctions. It's several pages long and...

The last page is not about the mafia. At the top, in Miss Berry's loopy handwriting, it says "My Perfect Husband: Specification".

I blink, and scan down the list in disbelief.

When I get to the final two items, my heart stops.

Seriously?

My pretty, innocent-looking assistant wants *that*?

I consider my options, or I tell myself that's what I'm doing. A gentleman would arrange it so she never knew I'd seen this. It's obviously private.

But being a mafia boss has its advantages. I am not a good man, I am a billionaire kingpin.

I pick up the phone before I can stop myself.

"Miss Berry. Could you come into my office for a moment?"

"Of course!" she sings out, but there's a tremor in her voice.

I only have to wait a few seconds and she's here, flushed, and her perfect hair has tendrils falling over her cheek.

"Close the door." I direct, and when she unhesitatingly does what I tell her, it should be sufficient to feed my addiction. It should. For six months I've told myself it's enough to have her working in the office next door, safe.

I still haven't decided what to do about this list, but Miss Berry is as red as her namesake.

"What's the matter?"

"Nothing!" she chirps in a way that absolutely means "something, but I'd rather die than tell you about it".

Inwardly, I sigh. I'd like to be the type of person she could confide in. I'd give anything to get into that little brain of hers. I'd like to know what she thinks, examine all her ideas and understand her desires. I want to insert myself into her every thought, so she feels some of the obsession I have with her.

If she just considered me as a man, not Mr Streatham, as she's always at pains to call me. If that sharp mind of hers could develop filthy fantasies for us to play out.

And maybe, just maybe, she has given me a way of suggesting that I could be more to her than a boss. Because I may not know anything about marriage and love, but I recognise an opportunity. And this?

I might be an accident, but on paper, I fit.

Picking up her handwritten husband list, I hold it so she can see.

She blinks, her chest heaving underneath that cute, prim little top that has my cock hardening.

I'm a master at weaponizing silence, and I do it now.

I raise one eyebrow and allow her to fill in what my thoughts might be about what she has written. In particular: five children.

Oh *yes*. Why stop at five?

3

SOPHIA

The blood drains from my whole body like I sprung a leak in my foot. I might faint.

My boss read my *perfect husband list*.

The list I wrote as I daydreamed about him, and describes him right down to age, facial hair choices, and eye colour.

"I'm so sorry." I go to snatch it from his hand, but he whips it out of my reach.

My mind reels through what he must have read.

Oh god. Now would be a great time for me to spontaneously combust. In fact, I think that's what my cheeks are doing. My body is so embarrassed it's trying to burn down the office. Perhaps smoke will pour from my burning limbs, the fire alarm will go off, and I can run away down the emergency stairs, out into London, never to be seen again.

"You wrote this?" he asks, with the absolute calm that I both hate and love and admire him for.

"That's not what it says it is." I squirm, but the lie is out of my mouth instinctively. Mr Streatham knowing about my pathetic crush on him is too awful. He's so out of my league he's practically on a different planet. "I was brainstorming. I was about to change half of it."

His eyes narrow, and for the smallest moment I think I see disappointment in his face. Then he's all grumpy arrogance again. He looks down, and reads aloud.

"Black hair. Grey eyes. Good teeth. Nice smile. Over forty. Perfect hygiene."

That's not too bad. That's normal.

There's a pause and he taps his forefinger on the page as though counting the other points.

Big hands.

I should have added that to the list, but in my defence, I didn't know that strong hands with a scatter of dark hair and square wrists were such a turn-on until I met my boss.

"Large penis."

I try not to breathe. Can I become invisible through sheer willpower? Probably not, with the heat emitting from my face.

I wrote penis.

My boss read *penis*. Not even a good word like cock or dick. Not a discreet, deniable word like length, staff, or magic sword, because I crossed out "staff" like an absolute muppet.

Actually, I think "staff" is worse. It makes me sound like a girl in a Regency romance about to shock everyone in high society by taking a glove off or something. *Oh Mr Darcy! Ladies mustn't indicate the girth of a gentlemen's staff with their hand!* Combined with my replacing it with penis—the official least-sexy word for cock, except perhaps weenie or beef whistle—gives me all the sophisticated sex appeal of an armadillo putting on lipstick.

My poor cheeks. As Mr Streatham regards me, I'm a neon sign. I could be part of the red-light district.

Armadillo. Lipstick. Trying to be a slut.

Nailed it.

And yet, I know there's worse to come. Literally.

Mr Streatham regards the paper, his eyebrows reaching about halfway down his nose. I stand utterly still, attempting dignity in this situation of day-time-Japanese-gameshow level of humiliation.

"High sperm count," he says, slowly enunciating every word.

Ah... Yes. There it is. The stupidest thing I have ever done, and that includes when I mixed up organism and orgasm in a presentation to my biology class.

"Miss Berry, why were you writing such a list, and how did it end up on my desk?" His tone is mild, almost neutral.

I consider saying, "For fun, I'm bored of life, and this seemed like a good way to go."

"What is this about?" he prompts me again and his deep voice resonates inside me.

"It's a list for a matchmaker," I admit miserably. "I applied to have an arranged marriage."

"You want a *marriage* of convenience?" Mr Streatham snarls. "You're too young to be getting married."

"I'm twenty-three. Old enough." I might blush so red I'll taint the whole of London pink, but that doesn't mean I have to back down.

"Why?" There's restrained fury in that one word.

The answer is simple. Because no one will ever love me.

"Arranged marriages are common in other parts of the world. We shouldn't be closed-minded." I try to be confident.

"Why, Miss Berry." His voice is dangerously soft, and he leans back into his chair, unblinking.

I gulp and clasp my hands together to prevent myself

from fidgeting as I tell myself I don't have to defend myself. He's my boss, but this is private.

There's a long, long silence as we look at each other.

It won't be me that breaks.

Never.

Those metal eyes don't relent, staring into me, bright and cold.

Mr Streatham is impossible to resist.

"It's not about the marriage," I admit finally.

"You're trying to get married but it's not about marriage. Explain."

"To have a baby." Right after the confession, I want to bite my tongue off. What is it about Mr Streatham that turns me into an idiot?

Oh, right. Hot, older, powerful mafia boss.

"Why not have IVF? Do I not pay you enough?"

"You do, you do." I'm paid very well by the Streatham mafia, and I'm grateful. "I just…"

If I think my boss will let this go, or make it easier on me, I'm dead wrong. He's intent on extracting the most humiliation. He isn't even blinking, and although his jaw is clenched, his hands are now relaxed, loosely clasped.

Ugh. This is why I deal with paperwork and not the more physical aspects of the Streatham mafia.

"I want my baby to have a father!" I burst out. I'd be useless as a spy.

His jaw unclenches. "Because you didn't."

And of all the things that have happened today, his three words might be the most embarrassing revelation of all.

He's seen me. I'm stripped bare. I have the crazy instinct to cover myself, but I'm wearing a top and a skirt perfectly appropriate for the office. I'm not naked, but with a single comment my boss has removed all my pretence of being a full adult making her own decisions, and exposed the worried little girl I'm always trying not to be.

Because, yes. I didn't have a dad. I was the product of a one-night stand. My mother never contacted my father, or had another relationship. It was her and me against the world, until when I was twenty, it wasn't her and me, it was just me.

Alone.

I open my mouth to tell my boss that I don't come to work to be psychoanalysed, and that the absence of a father figure in my life has nothing to do with my feelings about wanting a proper family with at least one backup parent for my child in case something happens to me, or crushing on a man old enough to be my father, and that he can get stuffed and this is none of his business.

But instead, I say, "How do you..."

"You told me."

For a second, I think I blurted out in a fever dream that I'm sad I don't have a father, and I want my boss to be the man who protects and loves me. Then my brain catches up, and I remember a late night at the office—the paper files mean working from home isn't a thing for the Streatham mafia—and he asked if anyone would be worried. He asked if I needed to phone my father, or a boyfriend.

And my heart sank to my toes as I said, no. There was no one waiting for me.

"You remember."

"I remember," he replies soberly. His gaze levels on my face. "Fine. Marriage it is."

"I wasn't asking for your permission," I mutter and lean quickly across the desk and scoop up my insane wish list.

It's not realistic and I'll have to scrap it, but I'm not leaving it with my boss.

His hand shoots out, quick as a snake bite, and grabs my wrist.

I gasp and try to pull back, but my little arm is no match for his rugged grip, his tendons bulging as he holds me in place.

His grasp is hard. Tight enough to hurt, just a bit, and my body responds with another flush of pink that I feel to my toes.

That sting of pain? Him holding me? His absolute dominance and the way I'm prone over his desk? All these things heat me between the legs. I'm instantly swollen and slick and needy.

My chin jerks up to look at him, and I'm totally at a disadvantage here.

He glowers down at me.

"I'll marry you."

"What?" All the blushing has overloaded my brain.

"I fit all the requirements on your list."

I gape. I don't think I heard him correctly.

"Well." He releases my wrist, and I scramble upright, facing him with the desk between us again. "Except one."

"The..." I can't bring myself to say the word. Because there are only two things that I didn't know for sure were true of Mr Streatham. "Size issue?"

"In a way." His silver eyes gleam.

"I should never have written that," I babble. I really imagined, having noticed at the uh, cut of his trousers, that he was big all over. "It was a stupid thing—"

"I don't turn forty until July," he cuts in.

Ohhh... I saw his date of birth written down and thought the month was a 1. It was not a 1. It was a 7.

"You're not yet forty," I whisper.

"Thirty-nine."

He meets all requirements except one, and that's his age. And there are two items that I didn't observe directly from him. Both to do with his... reproductive equipment.

"Be assured, Miss Berry," he says, looking me up and down, and presumably able to read me like I'm that list. I'm obviously figuring out the inference of what he said, and he's amused by it. "I have a very large *staff*."

My face heats again. "I, uh."

Any capacity to make words is steamrolled by talking to my boss about the size of his dick, after—and don't quote me on this because I'm still not certain I understood it correctly —he offered to marry me.

"Do I need to prove that?"

"No!"

His lips twitch. "I haven't measured, but it's at least seven..."

My brain fills in inches and I almost faint. That's very large. Very, very big indeed.

How would it fit?

How would it feel stretched so open if it did go in?

"Thousand people," he finishes smoothly. "I can call HR and check?"

I'm scarlet.

"No," I whimper. I'm going to need a new job because this is too much. He's teasing me. Perhaps I should resign right now?

"I suppose you're worried about the *other thing*," he continues.

Oh.

My. God.

Sperm count. It rebounds on me like a hair elastic

pinging on your hand when you're not paying attention doing a ponytail.

"Yes." Did I just accuse my kingpin boss of having a low sperm count? Crap, no. "I mean, no. I mean..."

"I'll prove it."

"A sperm sample?" The image of Mr Streatham with his cock in his hand, jerking off, groaning, the head of his huge cock going purple-red as he spurts white creamy seed into a tub and then hands it over to me, fills my mind.

If he gave it to me, still warm from his body, would I actually send it for sampling? Or would I... Taste it. See how it looked on my skin. My hands, my face, my breasts...

I never knew I had such a vivid imagination.

"Absolutely not," he says flatly.

No. Right. Obviously.

"But if..." I'm not sure what I'm saying here, since I cannot shake the image of Mr Streatham's come and what it would feel like smeared over me.

"If my swimmers aren't up to the job?" He taps his fingers on the desk impatiently. "They are."

"You have kids already?" My tummy slumps. I really do not like the thought of my boss with another woman, ever.

"No," he replies firmly. "No. I don't have any children."

"But you want kids?"

He leans forwards, suddenly much more intense. I can almost feel the heat from his body, burning me. His gaze strays down to my midriff and lingers there.

Is he imagining me pregnant with his baby?

"Yes, darling. I want children. I'll give you children."

Hooded eyes meet mine again and I melt. Darling. He called me darling.

And he wants me to have his babies. My suddenly inventive mind sees black-haired, hazel-eyed kids laughing as they play on Streatham Common. I see my boss spinning around a little girl with soft brown hair and grey eyes like his own.

"But it would be like an arranged marriage? No expectations of love," I say faintly. "A sort of marriage of convenience?"

He dips his chin in assent.

It was me who came up with the idea, and so I can't expect love, and yet my stomach lurches as though I've walked all the way up the stairs and expected another step.

Because being a wife to a stranger would be one thing. There wouldn't be any feelings on either side, and I could get on with being a mother without love muddying the relationship.

But with Dexter Streatham, that's impossible. There's no chance of me being happy with just having his children and being his convenient wife.

It would hurt far too much.

I love him. The whole reason for this arranged marriage idea was to get over my feelings for my boss, so my heart didn't tap-dance every time I saw him, not trap me in a lifelong situation where I pine for his affection but never have it.

So for the sake of my sanity, I have to top my most stupid action again today. Sorry organism and orgasm, you're relegated to third place.

"I can't marry you."

4

DEX

She will. She absolutely will marry me.

The alternative is unthinkable. Another man, having Sophia?

No.

"Thank you for the offer, if it was that." She tilts up her chin. "But I'm going to use *London Matchmakers*."

Jealous rage rises in me like a fire sparking into life.

I assumed she wasn't interested in marriage and children, since my previous assistant picked her out and I'm a demanding boss. I require absolute commitment, and I pay generously for it.

But if she's marrying? Even though I'm too old for her, and she's too sweet for me, she'll be mine.

If I were a good man, I would let this go.

"Why?" I snap.

"Because…" She hesitates, all the certainty of a moment ago seeping away. "Two reasons."

"Which are."

"Good reasons." Nodding, she wipes her hands on her

skirt and presses her lips together. She's stalling, and it's unlike her. Usually Miss Berry is serene and organised.

I give her time to think up her spurious excuses because I like that I'm seeing a different side to her.

"Safety," she says after a few seconds. "He wouldn't be a mafia boss. The London mafias are dangerous."

"Are you suggesting I couldn't take care of my family," I reply slowly.

"No." She gulps and quickly backtracks, twisting her hands together.

Nervous. No wonder. That's a nonsense reason, and we both know it.

"Second, I want children. That's important. A sperm sample will ensure the best possible chance, and you've refused to that." She becomes steadier as she gets more confident of her reason. "I don't want to make you uncomfortable."

"I'll get you pregnant." I'll be dedicated to the pursuit. It's a given, as is our marriage. "We'll have all the children you want." She presumably thinks I'll be a terrible husband and father, and that's why she's reluctant. But I'll prove her wrong and do something absurdly sentimental to win her love.

Right after I look up romance in a reference book. I must have a book on this.

"I heard it can take ages." She twists her hands. "That you have to do all sorts of things to increase the chances."

If she thinks the idea of having sex repeatedly is off-putting, she couldn't be more wrong. I allow myself a glimpse of the future. Her, barefoot and pregnant, our toddler in her arms. She'd welcome me home after work, and we'd play games with our children and settle them into bed. Then I'd bend Sophia over the sofa and make her scream. She'd orgasm three times before I finally spill into her.

"And?"

"I want to get pregnant quickly. So I need a sperm sample."

A waste of time.

Alarm takes over her expression as I stand and go to the bookshelf. Pulling out a volume of the encyclopaedia—my girl is so young she probably thinks the only source of knowledge before Wikipedia was stone tablets—I open it to Fertility. Sliding reading glasses on and within a minute I have the key points.

"Less frequent ejaculation increases sperm concentration, so you'll be more likely to get pregnant."

She nods warily. "I heard that."

"The other critical aspect is when you're fertile. Where are you in your cycle?"

"I'm not talking to my boss about my menstrual cycle," she says primly, and I raise my eyebrows.

"But you are going to talk to your husband-to-be about it. Because he wants to get you pregnant." She has no idea how vital it is to me.

She makes a sound of dissent.

I just wait, regarding her levelly.

"It finished yesterday." She winces.

"That explains how ferociously you shredded those poor documents last week."

Covering her face with her hands, she groans. "Paper destruction is a healthy way to deal with PMS."

"That's basically what I do when I'm stressed too. But it's the other guy who bleeds." I check the chart of the fertility cycle.

She huffs with soft laughter.

"So you'll be ready to conceive in about ten days." I slam closed the book and push it back onto the shelf, then return to my desk, tossing the glasses off so I can see Sophia clearly.

Ten days until I can have her? That's forever. It is the lifespan of a star. Civilisations will rise and fall while I wait billions of years.

"You think that old book is correct?" she says uncertainly, removing her hands from her face.

Is she doubting my *books*? "I'd bet on it."

Her complicated eyes slip down and her eyelashes fan over her cheek. She's silent.

And for once, it's my tension that rises. I can't afford to let her go.

There's a moment when negotiating with a potential spy that you must choose how to close the deal. My usual methods are pain, a threat, blackmail, or a bribe. I mentally flick through the options, and reject each one.

Panic grips me. I can feel her slipping away. This matters so much more than anything I've achieved in my life before, and needs a different approach.

"I bet that I'll get you pregnant within six months."

It's an explosion of a statement into the quiet, and brings her gaze back to mine.

"And if you don't?" she asks warily.

"We'll do it a different way. Either a sperm donor, and I'll be the father, or we'll divorce, and I'll help you find someone else." It's a crazy impulse, but I'll risk anything to be with her.

"You'd really help me find another husband?"

No.

"Absolutely. If that's what you want." But she won't. I have a billion in the bank and a very enthusiastic tongue.

She'll be too busy either sitting on my face or using her credit card emblazoned with Mrs Sophia Streatham to consider leaving.

"Think of it like a money-back guarantee. If we divorced, you'd have half my fortune, too." And my whole bloody heart in her hands, so what's money in comparison.

Hopefully, she'll have a child nine months from now, but I have no intention of letting her go either way.

"I guess," she murmurs, sounding baffled.

"We'll get married as soon as possible, and start trying for a baby in ten days." If the price of having her forever is six months of frustration as I can only come when she'll conceive, well, what's the difference? I've been pining after my perfect little assistant for a long time already. At least now I'll get more of her.

Doubt still clouds her face, and she nibbles her lip.

I'm a billionaire mafia boss. It should not be this difficult to persuade a woman to marry me.

I wait.

Seconds drag past. I *will* win. She's not leaving this building without agreeing. This morning, I had no idea this would happen, but the thought of Miss Berry belonging to anyone but me has made me willing to cross any line.

If I have to lock her up, so be it.

"But why?" she bursts out eventually. "Why are you offering to marry me?"

Obviously, because I'm in love with her, and want to spend the rest of my life making her happy and pregnant, not accepting cups of coffee from her and wondering if any man has touched her and therefore needs to die. That is the reason people usually get married.

"I need this, too."

5

SOPHIA

"You need to get married?" I whisper, in shock.

I never thought I'd hear my gorgeous, severe boss casually talking about us having sex as though it were a work project, but marriage? That's insane. He could have any woman he wanted, and he's a billionaire mafia boss, what possible reason does he have to "need" to do anything?

He regards me for a moment, then rises from his chair and casually turns his back. Shoving his hands into his pockets, he stares out of the window onto the golden-yellow of the early afternoon sunshine.

He's framed as a dark silhouette in a black suit compared to the light outside, that slightly wavy dark hair highlighted. His neck is in shadow, and I have this sudden impulse to trace it with my finger.

I'm hot and squirmy at the thought of him *breeding* me. Such an animalistic term, I really shouldn't be turned on by it. But my body hasn't got the message that I'm not a creature made up of hormones, wet secret places waiting to be discovered, and stationary with doodles of hearts and Mrs Streatham written on it.

If the first time I had a man inside me was with the man I love, surely it would be worth it, especially if I was helping him?

But maybe it would only be once, just to give me a child?

That might break me.

"You know the London Maths Club?" he says eventually.

"You mean the London Mafia Syndicate," I say, but I'm thinking what it would be like to have him naked on top of me. Inside me.

Since I took over as his assistant, the London Mafia Syndicate has been a constant fixture of his schedule, with a combination of highly-sensitive negotiations and also charity balls and that sort of thing.

I still don't understand why sometimes it's called the London Maths Club, since they clearly don't do any mathematics.

He tilts his head in an action that doesn't mean yes or no. "There are social events for the wives too. Many of the most-influential mafia bosses are married, and unenthusiastic about bachelors."

"You don't fit in?" My chest aches at that. He might be rich and powerful and I'm nothing by comparison, but this feeling I know about. Being on the outside of the popular crowd.

"They're more welcoming to members who are married."

"So you want a marriage of convenience to fool them that you're the same?"

He makes the same tilt of the head, which I take to mean, yes.

He needs me.

How can I refuse? All the same reasons not to do this remain: I'm for sure going to be hurt beyond repair by being his wife, having sex with him to make babies, and never ever be able to get over my *crush*. But I think he'd be a good father. I'd have the children I so want, he'd have a token wife to smooth things with the London Mafia Syndicate.

Only my stupid feelings stand in the way of a good solution.

"Do you think you could fake some affection for me?" he asks huskily.

My mouth goes dry as I bore my gaze into the back of his head.

Fake? No.

But I could open up a few of the internal doors I keep locked, and reveal a small part of how far gone I am for my boss. Would he pretend to love me in return?

My little heart patters at the idea. Maybe we wouldn't let on to the London Mafia Syndicate that it was a marriage of convenience? Foolishly, I'd like that. Could we go to every meeting together? Three visits a day, preferably, so he always had to pretend.

"I think I could manage."

"Good girl." If I thought he'd sound relieved, or happy, I was mistaken. But good girl? I cover my mouth to suppress a gasp. Good girl. That's borderline pornographic. Is it even legal?

My clit throbs.

"Mr Streatham."

He nods.

"There's something I need to tell you." I didn't want to reveal this secret, especially not to my boss. But he's telling me the truth, confessing he's left out of the London Mafia Syndicate. And honesty is the basis of a good relationship, right?

So before he can turn, I tumble the words out.

"I'm a virgin."

6

DEX

I swing around, my heart making a bid for freedom via my mouth and ribcage simultaneously.

She cowers, as though I might be angry with her for saving her cherry for me. Nothing could be further from the truth. My sweet Miss Berry, giving me her first bite.

"You've never had sex." I feel I need to clarify this, because it's not every Tuesday afternoon that all your dreams come true. "Were you waiting for marriage?"

I thought I was the old-fashioned one, but was she keeping her first time for her husband to breach her on her wedding night?

"No, not really. I'm shy," she whispers. "I just didn't find the right person."

She has now, or if she hasn't that's bad luck. I *will* take her virginity.

Grey eyes. Tall. Rich. Short beard.

Look, it's probably as she said, a generic list. But she wouldn't have written those attributes down if they repulsed her, would she? No.

I can work with that. I'll get her addicted to the feel of my length inside her and orgasms from my hands.

And if I need to pretend that I'm left out of the London Mafia Syndicate in order to convince Sophia to marry me, that's what I'll do. It's not true, but not entirely a lie, either. I've gone from irritated by the number of vomit-inducingly happy couples that are part of that group to something very like jealous.

My virgin bride. Fuck. She has no idea she just made the next ten days impossibly hard. Hypothermia will be a constant risk with the number of cold showers I'm going to need. But I won't jerk off to remove the edge. It's critical we have a baby to tie us together permanently.

"We can take it slow and gentle," I reassure her. And I will. Even if it kills me.

"Oh." She twists her lips as she thinks. "The thing is, I don't want the only time I have sex to be when I get pregnant."

I nod slowly and sink back onto my chair, even as my heart does some sort of idiotic dance move. A jump, or a hop, or a flip.

"I want to learn about sex, so when I do get pregnant it won't be a second-place event to sex being new. I'll be able to appreciate..." She covers her face with her hands. "Oh this is ridiculous! Forget I said anything."

"Enjoying getting pregnant for its own sake, not just the sex."

She peeks around her hands. "Yes. Is that weird?"

My girl has a breeding kink, and hell, I didn't think she could be any better matched to me, but this goes to show how limited my view was.

"It's not weird to me."

"So you don't mind?" Lowering her hands, she regards me anxiously.

"You want to practise and learn?" I will teach her. No problem.

"But you said no sex." She bites her lip.

"Is that what I said, darling?"

"But..." Poor confused girl, she blinks, trying to figure it out.

"We can have sex without me emptying my balls into you and filling you up with my seed."

The gasp like she's a maiden in a period drama is belied by a hint of a smile at the corner of her mouth.

Once she's my wife, I'll take pleasure in getting her pregnant. Until then, I will make it so good she can't see straight.

"You're going to marry me." It's a question, or at least, she interprets it that way, and nods. "Then let's start your lessons."

"Now?" she squeaks.

"Come here."

She pauses.

"You can lock the door first." There's no chance of anyone interrupting us, but I intend to see a lot of my assistant and I won't have any shyness. I push back in my office chair, and watch her as she turns the key. She's so sexy, I don't think she has any idea how fucking hot she is in that demure outfit that tries to hide everything but makes her an intriguing present.

"What about...?" She glances over at the windows.

I nod slowly. "Close the blinds."

Sophia is methodical, and my cock is getting harder by the second. She returns to her place before my desk instead of coming to me, and I'm momentarily disappointed. I want her on my lap.

I lean back in my chair.

"Show me what a good girl you'll be as I breed you."

She blinks. "How?"

"Take off your clothes," I demand hoarsely, and I think it surprises me as much as it does her.

Her hands tremble as she reaches for the hem of her top.

Then it's my turn to shake as she pulls it over her head, exposing a plain white bra and perfect skin. I grip the arms of my chair to prevent me from going over right then and mauling her.

"Go on," I say with more calm than I feel.

Her skirt drops after the longest seconds of my life and she's there like a sweet, corruptible angel, in white cotton panties and that simple bra.

"Very good." My voice definitely gives me away this time as she regards me from under her lashes, her blush tinting her chest with pink. I bet her nipples are gorgeous little berries.

"What should I do now, Mr Streatham?"

Fuck, the breathy way she says my name hardens my cock more than believed possible.

"Sit here." My knuckles almost break as I remove one hand from the chair arm and slap my thigh.

She's heaven as she approaches around my desk, slips off her shoes, and then stops as her gaze angles down at my lap.

I'm sporting a massive hard-on.

"Ignore that for now. Sit across my knees."

There's a tentativeness in her movements that I want to end

forever. Part of me that dares to dream that one day we'll do this sort of thing, and she'll push me back and eagerly straddle me to take what she's owed, or kneel to cover me with her mouth.

That day is not today. She sits gingerly, as though trying not to be too heavy.

"Miss Berry."

"Yes."

I love you and I want this to be everything for you, as it's going to be for me.

"Forget that this is a marriage of convenience for a moment."

She huffs sceptically.

"And that we're in my office."

"And it's a Tuesday afternoon." She looks over at me and that little edge of sass that I adore is playing at the corner of her mouth.

"Right now, all that matters is this." I hold my breath as I take her nearest hand and guide it up to my shoulder, so she leans into me. "I'm your fiancé. I'm going to give you a baby if you're a good girl, and practice very well."

"Yeah. That's..." She swallows and nods. "Sensible."

I reach for her other hand and bring it up, so we're palm to palm. We both look down at our hands.

Hers is tiny compared to mine, with smooth, creamy skin. My rougher knuckles with black hair at my wrist make me seem exactly the opposite of her lightness. My cock throbs. She's dainty and small, and I simultaneously want to crush and ravish and protect her.

"Kiss me." It comes out a growl, and she freezes.

"Come on, fiancée," I taunt her softly. My lips are tingling with how much I want this.

"Uughgh." She wriggles and looks down, and her cute,

peachy bottom almost touches my rigid cock. We both stop moving.

A second ticks past.

"I don't know how," she confesses.

"You've never kissed anyone?"

"I have, but not..." She shakes her head. "Not recently."

"Been busy?"

"School, university, work. It's a lot." She shrugs and I brush my thumb over hers. "And my latest job is far too hectic to have time for dating."

"Sorry." There isn't a hint of sincerity in that word. "Your boss will make up for it."

Her gaze flicks down again. "When you said 'staff', I didn't expect..."

"I know." She thought I was exaggerating. I wasn't. "We'll get to that. A kiss first."

Those pretty, hazel eyes, like a dappled summer forest, melt into trust and she eases closer and closer, until I'm almost cross-eyed. Then her soft lips brush mine.

It's exactly the sort of kiss I'd have expected from her. Gentle and hesitant, as though she thinks she could hurt me.

"Your beard..." she says, drawing back.

"You want me to shave it off?" I tighten my hand around hers.

"No." She leans in. "I like it," she whispers, and kisses me again. I let her explore, slowly, then begin to guide her. I nibble, and urge her lips apart to slip my tongue inside in an echo of what I'm going to do to her soon. And this time, she doesn't pull away. Not when one of my hands finds her waist and pulls her close, pressing her tummy against my erection. Not when my other hand slides into her hair and tightens, pulling it just enough to make her gasp before she presses her mouth harder onto mine, so the tension increases.

Everything about her is silk. Her hair that's falling out of that neat up-do, her skin. Even the edge of those innocent cotton knickers.

We kiss for a long time, until she's making whimpering sounds, and her hands are sneaking under my suit jacket and tracing over my neck. I take that as permission to start my own exploration of her body. The soft curve of her waist, the graceful plane of her shoulders. I have to bite back a moan as I cup her little tits. Every caress makes me need her more.

When we break our kiss, both gasping for air, I glimpse my hand on her ribcage and the contrast is obscene. Underneath this expensive suit, I'm coarse and heavy. Whereas without her pretty clothes, she's fragile and beautiful as a butterfly.

I sweep both hands up and down her torso and it's almost too much. I don't deserve all of her goodness on my lap like this, but I'm a selfish bastard and I'll take it.

For six months only, if I lose my bet.

Shit, I cannot think about that.

Instead, I bring my hands to her hips.

"Say yes, little one. Say you want my big, brutish fingers in your virgin pussy to get you ready for my cock." My tone is harsh, almost trying to put off.

Her response is to wriggle closer. She's worked her way around so she's practically sitting face-to-face with me, and I'm so greedy I still need more. Her words.

"Tell me what you want, little one," I rasp.

"I can't say those things!" she whispers.

"Say, 'touch me where a man of almost forty shouldn't touch his pretty, twenty-three-year-old assistant'." My desperation is increasing and making me filthy. "Say, 'Please teach me about sex'."

"Please touch my virgin pussy, Mr Streatham."

Oh fuuckk. Precome leaks out of my cock. I'm going to have to go slow when I make love to my girl, because I could easily shoot off too soon and ruin my chance of getting her pregnant. And that is the only important thing. Give her the baby and family she wants, so I can keep her.

"Dexter. Call me Dex." I sound like I've run a marathon. "Streatham will be your name very soon."

"Please put your fingers inside me, Dex." Her breathy voice asking me to defile her is hot beyond my wildest dreams.

I slide my fingers down her abdomen and into her underwear. I think how it will get firm and swollen with my baby, then lower, lower. Over her mons, then down, and then... That hidden flower is open for me.

My fingertips meet a drop of moisture, then more. She's slippery.

"You're wet." I breathe the revelation in disbelief. She wants this. The prickle of unease that I was seducing her disappears, the relief instant like pulling out a splinter.

"I..." She tries to hide from me, glancing away.

"No." I grab her chin with my other hand and turn her, so she has to face me. "It's a good thing, little one. You're such a good girl. But I was looking forward to licking you to get you ready to take me."

Her tongue nips out and moistens those other perfect, plush lips and I suppress a moan. How did I survive six months of working with my assistant without bending her over my desk?

"Sorry?" Her tone has a hint of cute brattiness.

"And you're not robbing me of that honour."

Dragging her mouth to mine, I touch our lips together in a deceptively sweet kiss. I hope she remembers that, because I'm about to be ruthless.

I wrap my arms around her waist, and continue kissing her as I lift her up. She gasps and holds on, and I purr in approval as I set her on my desk, amongst all the papers, trailing kisses over her jaw.

I'm fucking starving, and I have to eat. I have to get my mouth on her.

I can't come, but I want her to quake like I'm a force of nature. Like I'm shattering her and making her anew. I reach her chest, and the swell of her tits makes me feral. Shoving the cup of her practical bra aside, I suck her nipple into my mouth. And my sweet girl moans, grabbing my head and I didn't think I could enjoy this any more than I was already, but yeah that'll do it.

I worship her breasts as they deserve, and caress her back, and arse, and sides with my hands until she's shaking and murmuring my name.

"Dex."

"Take your knickers off," I order her, not breaking contact with her skin. I don't sound like myself. I'm hanging on by a thread and my cock is trying to break out of my trousers.

"Yes, Mr Streatham." Within seconds she's managed to wriggle out of her underwear, and I drag it down her long legs and stuff the trophy into my pocket. My fingers dig into both her knees as I lower myself, watching her surprised expression as I push her thighs apart.

Then I look down.

"Fuuuck, little one."

"What is it?" she asks, with a hint of worry.

"You're so pretty everywhere. But here?" I can hardly breathe. "Sophia, you're perfect."

Virginity is a concept I've never cared about before, and hymen is an ugly word. But Sophia rewrites every rule for me. I am so possessive of this girl. I want to claim her like an animal would his mate, with a bite, covering her with my scent, and getting her round with my offspring.

Tucked in the middle of her soft pink, slick folds is my prize. Her bud of a clit is swollen with need. And below, her entrance is tiny, and the edge of her hymen smooth. I'll be the one to stretch her out. She's *mine*.

I drag my gaze from her pussy for a second to find her wide-eyed.

"I'm going to lick you until you come all over my face," I tell her firmly. "To get you ready to take my cock."

7

DEX

She seems mildly shocked as she replies, "Okay."

"Good girl."

I take my time with the first lick all the way up her slit, and I'm not sure what's better: the taste of her honey, the little panting sounds she makes, or how she shudders. More sampling needed to be certain. I lick her again, and yeah, those noises are sweet as fuck as I go over her clit. She's delicious, but as I focus my attention and tongue on that sensitive place, I can't help but grin at the way she writhes and moans.

Gripping her thighs and pushing her wider open for me, I gorge on her softness. She's a total contrast to me. My cock is leaking pre-come, desperate and unable to wait any longer to get inside her. But I'll wait, because her needs are more important right now. Meanwhile, she's dripping her sweet liquid out, covering my beard with it and getting us both sloppy.

A glance upwards reveals that her eyes are hazy and she's leaning back on her arms. She's flushed again and those lovely nipples are pert for me. I look forward to getting back to sucking them, but for now, I keep my tongue rhythmically flicking over her clit, again and again, driving her higher.

Reluctantly letting go of one of her thighs, I stroke all the way down her leg, then back up. Next to where I'm licking her, I gently press the tip of my forefinger into where she's dripping onto my table. There's a bit of resistance, then she stretches for me, and I push in. She's hot and tight.

"Oh-my-god-oh-my-god-Dex-Dex," she babbles.

"That's it, open," I say between sucks on her clit, then go further, gradual but unrelenting, withdrawing and going deeper.

"Dex, I... That feels..."

I pause, my finger in as far as the third knuckle.

"No!"

I'm about to pull away when her hand finds the back of my head and clamps onto me.

"No, don't stop. Please, Dex. Don't stop."

At your service, little one.

Sucking harder on her throbbing bundle of nerves, I curl my finger up and drag it out before shoving back in, fast this time, and she moans, grip tightening in my hair.

Then it's a steady increase, my hand and tongue working together. She begins to lose control, and I chase her, ravenous for her to peak with my face pushed into her folds.

It's gratifyingly easy for me to break her. She comes, shuddering and clenching and holding onto me. She pulses around my finger in wave after wave of pleasure and I'm so proud I could shout or sing or take out a front-page ad in *The Times*. "My good virgin girl came for me," would make quite the headline.

I work her through it with kisses and slow slides, and

enjoy how slick she is. And yeah, I think about how that tight, wet heat is going to feel on my cock. Heaven.

When she's finally still, I push to my feet and look down at my girl, spread on my desk. With Sophia half reclined, I tower over her, but her cunt is at exactly the right height. She's temptation incarnate, sprawled amongst the papers, her tits falling out of her bra, a sheen of sweat on her skin, and her legs open like a needy little slut. For me. She's a slut for *me*.

With shaking hands as though this is my first time too, I free my cock. I'm unable to do more than shove the necessary clothing aside, not even undress.

This feels fresh. Different. I'm going to take her virginity and that's new to me. I love her, and she's the only one who has ever caused this spiralling in my chest. I've never needed a woman so much that I can't wait long enough to get to a bed, and we're in my goddamned office on a weekday afternoon. And there is no one as beautiful as Sophia.

So I guess it's not a surprise that this feels like I'm a virgin as well, and as eager to have my bride as she is for me.

Sophia's eyes flutter open and fixate on where my cock juts obscenely from my open trousers.

"You're so big," she breathes.

She knows all the right things to say. And I'm a bastard, because I enjoy that thread of fear in her voice. She's a virgin, and she's going to take all of my massive cock.

"Wasn't that what you wanted?" I tease her, hiding my glee. "You put it on your list, remember?"

"Please do not remind me of the worst embarrassment of my life," she replies with a wince.

"You said you wanted a man with—"

"I know what I wrote," she cuts me off. "And I'm still dying of embarrassment."

"Well." I straighten and take my cock in my hand, stroking up and down. Her gaze dips to my shaft again. "Having seen it up close, are you going to change your list?"

"No. No, I... Please, Dex." Her eyes meet mine. "Please."

"So pretty when you beg," I murmur with a smirk I can't suppress, then pause. "This might hurt." I'd accept all her pain myself if I could. "Just the first time."

"I know. That's partly why I didn't want this to be when I get pregnant. In case I..." She sighs. "Bottle it and never want to do it again, and then it'll be a terrible experience."

"It won't be." I swear that as I angle my cock down and slide it over her wet slit, covering the swollen head with her slick. It sends a bolt of pleasure from where we touch.

I notch myself at her entrance then narrow my eyes as I notice she's just watching me, passive. And I look at the distance between our faces, and the lack of intimacy. I can't even kiss her like this.

That won't do.

"Come here." I scoop her up with one arm and lift her, then step back and settle into my office chair, and I'm thankful it's big enough for her to have her knees on the leather either side of my thighs.

She steadies herself with her hand on my shoulders and blinks at me. "I thought you were going to..."

"Fuck you on my desk?" I finish for her. "I was. But you want to learn about sex?" I run my hand over her head and down her neck, settling one hand over her collarbone and the other on her heart, then gently pull her forwards to speak into her ear. "You should do this for yourself. Explore.

Use me. I'm here. Whatever you decide to try, I'll do. And you can take this at your own pace."

She looks down at where my aching cock is wedged between us. Dragging in a shaky breath, she pushes up, and she's small enough compared to me that I only have to tilt my chin up an inch as she's on her knees before me. I hold my cock for her and guide her down, and the moment the head presses into where she's wet and warm and yielding, I exhale with relief.

I've *needed* this. I want to tell her so as she balances herself and whimpers as she works herself down with the help of gravity.

"That's it," I encourage her, instead of scaring her with my obsession. "Take what's yours."

"It pinches," she says with a quaver in her tone.

"I know, I know." I stroke down her side, over her belly, and down to where I'm splitting her. "But it's going to feel amazing." It already does for me. "You're doing so well. Such a good girl."

The praise emboldens her, and she lowers again, taking an inch, then slowly, gradually, another inch.

"Fuck. Fuucccck." I try to breathe through the surge of pleasure. "You're tight. So tight."

"Sorry," she says awkwardly, and I half laugh, half groan as her forehead creases with concern.

"No, it's a good thing, little one." I push the tendril of hair that has fallen out of whatever she does with it to keep it up away from her pretty face. "You feel amazing."

"Oh." She blinks. "Too much? Should I stop? In case you..."

I shake my head and catch the back of her neck, bringing her lips to me. Never. She should never leave me.

Kissing her is good, because it prevents me from saying

more as she returns to lifting and lowering herself on my length. If I can't speak because I'm kissing her, I won't tell her that I love her, or that this might be a marriage of convenience but that I'm never letting her go, or that it's going to kill me holding on until she's most fertile.

I also can't confess that I don't need her as enhanced credibility for the London Maths Club. It was the only slightly plausible reason I could think of, that wasn't that she's captivated me, body and soul, since we met.

"You're mine, now," I say hoarsely, losing the promise into her skin in a low murmur. She mustn't hear. She'd run from me, and I couldn't bear that. "You belong to me from this day forward."

Having her the first time is a primal claim unlike anything I've experienced.

She lifts herself off a bit, then slides back down and I help her, guiding her hips and murmuring praise.

"I'm going to stroke your clit again, little one," I say when she's getting the hang of it. "I want you to come on my cock." I want to feel her ecstasy, and I'm just praying I can hold on, and not let her tip me over.

Her gaze flies to mine. "I don't know if I can."

"You're capable of amazing things." I reach to where she's slippery between her legs and when I touch her, she tightens, drawing a moan from me. Her inexperience is making it slightly easier to not come, but if she milks it out of me...

I focus on her face, not allowing my gaze to drop to where her tits are bouncing, or where her cream is seeping out and covering the base of my cock and dribbling onto my heavy balls.

"You're so tight. That's it, little one." I circle over her clit, watching her carefully for any sign it's too much. But there's none. She's gasping and panting, holding onto my shoulders as she uses me.

"You're enormous. You're—ohhh!" Her eyes flutter closed and for a few seconds I allow the tenderness and love in my heart to show in my face as I watch her come.

"My beautiful darling. Go on. You've earned it." I move to touching the edge of her clit and rubbing her back as she collapses, grinding down on my length, taking as much as she can. "Come on this big cock you've managed so bravely."

I can feel pre-come pushing up from the tip of my cock, and I don't know whether to hope for more, on the smallest off-chance it could get her pregnant, or wish it would stay entirely in my balls, waiting for the prime moment.

What I do know is my bride's place is on me, like this.

Sophia makes an "mm" sound and lifts herself slowly up, resuming her slide over my cock, her breath hitching.

She's so lovely, discovering her dormant sexuality with me and I admire her.

The phone rings, a jarring, shrill noise cutting into our moment.

We both look at it.

Sophia is naked, riding my cock. I'm still fully dressed apart from where we're joined.

Damnit, I've only just felt her perfect soft wet channel over my length after a lifetime of being without her. I need more.

I'm not ready for this to end yet.

"It's the London Maths—I mean Mafia Syndicate group call," she whispers, as though she might accidentally summon them into the room. "I should go—"

"No." I grip her as she begins to shift off me. "Stay."

Her patterned eyes meet mine. "What are you saying?"

The phone continues to ring.

"Ten days, little one. We only have ten days for you to practise." Because what if she gets pregnant immediately? She might not want to do it again, or something else could go wrong. I need to make the most of every opportunity.

"And you think this will help?" There are nerves in her expression, yes, but arousal too.

"Can you be my good, quiet girl?" I'll protect her. Have one thumb ready to hang up at any moment. But this is her choice, so I relax my grip. "Just keep me warm for a bit until we can get back to what we were doing."

A long beat of quiet is punctuated by the insistent shrill of the phone, and I'm certain she's going to leave.

The ring is so loud. It's intrusive into our silent communication between our bodies. I'm trying not to beg with my eyes, because my cock is doing that eloquently. I'm harder than ever, even though she's stopped moving.

But after a gulp, she nods and the dark thrill of the risk of what we're doing pulses in my bloodstream.

"Sit still for me, darling." I allow myself a smug smile as I pick up the call. "Streatham here."

"Bloody took your time about it," Lambeth grumbles, and a few others give equally surly greetings before Westminster snaps and begins to talk business.

For a few minutes, she just sits on my lap, and I relish the taboo of what we're doing. I have my young, gorgeous, forbidden, assistant on me. Her naked tits are right in my eyeline, and every little wriggle of her bottom sends sparks from the crown down to my balls.

My virgin employee. During work time.

That in itself is filthy, but having my cock soaking inside of her during a meeting? Absolutely degraded, and I love it.

I lean fully back into the padded leather of the chair, and listen to the updates, phone in one hand.

Sophia is wide-eyed and disbelieving, but squirming a bit. She's a kinky little thing, getting off on this casual-use vibe. Is it me using her, or her using me? It's sort of both.

With slow deliberation, I bring my hand to her breast, and slowly explore the area as though I have no end in mind.

"Streatham," Westminster barks. "What about Operation Calculus? Do you have an update on the situation with the Essex Cartel?"

Sophia is motionless.

"We're making very good progress," I say, looking my girl in the eye, and roll her nipple. "Very good indeed."

She arches, pushing her small breasts towards me.

"Are we talking about the same thing?" Mayfair demands, his Russian accent stronger with annoyance.

"We had a slight inconvenience," I reply, "But we've fixed it now." Or rather, I will fix my girl up with a baby. Reaching for her clit, I gently begin to circle where she's most sensitive.

Sophia bites her lip and squirms as I methodically coax her higher and explain the problem I had with my Essex Cartel sources to the rest of the Syndicate.

"And you're sure you can trust David Tiptree?" grumbles the Canary Wharf kingpin.

"Yes." Looking into Sophia's hazel eyes, I say, "I have no doubts."

Westminster speaks, fussing about the potential for failure, and I barely listen.

"Touch your breasts," I mouth. Then I have to suppress a groan as Sophia does as I bid, and the sight of her pinching her nipple nearly makes me shoot my load right into her, up against her womb where it's needed.

"We need to ensure we move at the correct time, and don't reveal ourselves to the Essex Cartel." I raise my eyebrows meaningfully to my little assistant, even as I ruthlessly rub her clit.

There's a noisy discussion about the best way to keep our activities in the Essex Cartel secret.

Her expression is one of surprise and drugged with pleasure as she lifts herself just an inch then pushes back down on my cock, almost entirely silent. Her mouth is open in a pant. She's close, and it fills me with pride stronger than anything I've felt before.

This girl is going to have my baby. Be by my side, and, if how she's responding to my touch is an indication, be in my bed.

"Yes, perfect..."

"What's perfect?" Mayfair snaps.

I curse inwardly. My future wife bouncing on my cock, that's what's perfect. "Securing the plan."

She tightens around me and lets out a squeak as she works herself on my length. I have to close my eyes for a second to avoid spilling right there.

The phone call recedes. The world narrows down to this woman, and the way she feels. All my concentration is on getting her to her climax. London could burn to the ground for all I care.

She covers her mouth with her hand as the orgasm wracks through her.

I grit my teeth as her tight little passage tries to milk me.

"Something's come up," I say abruptly, and slam the phone down. Catching Sophia's chin with two fingers, I lift it until she's looking into my eyes.

"We'll do that every day. As many times as you like, so you're ready to be bred."

8

SOPHIA

Today's workday done list:

Three orgasms, tick.

Lost my virginity, tick.

Got engaged to my boss, tick.

Nearly died of heatstroke caused by my own cheeks, tick.

Boring paperwork, tick.

Overall: best day of my life. I'm a dog being given steak after a lifetime of dry kibble.

Between my legs still feels... Different. Stretched and tingly and new. The other part of me that's altered is my tummy. It's alternately full of butterflies and lead. What am I going to do? I was supposed to be getting married and having a baby to forget my crush on my boss, and instead I've said I'll be tied to him forever, pretending to be a happy couple, watching him father our children, all the time knowing he doesn't return my love.

But he needs me.

Sure, it's only with fitting in better with the Maths Club

kingpins, but that's enough. It's heady. Mr Streatham, billionaire and mafia boss, needs *me*.

Yes, it's fake, and yes, it'll hurt when he gets bored, or strays, or becomes tired of faking with his wife and decides to...

I cannot think about that.

The orgasms he gave me, they didn't feel fake. And Mr Streatham inside me? More decadent than expensive chocolate, better than getting full marks on a test. More swoony than my favourite book.

I think about it for the rest of the afternoon as I work. I don't see Mr Streatham. He's in his office, and I'm out here with my rising anxiety and newly needy pussy.

I don't usually see my boss all the time, but between him not calling me to get him a cup of tea or pull this or that file as he normally would, my worry mounts. It creeps towards five o'clock with all the haste of my favourite author writing the last instalment of the series after a massive cliffhanger.

Normally, he asks me to work late because my standard working hours are nine until five. So when it's four-fifty-nine, I'm about ready to vomit with nerves.

He's ignoring me.

Does he wish this hadn't happened? Maybe I should just pretend I didn't give myself to him, heart and soul and first times, on his desk? Go home, eat an entire family-sized bar of chocolate, watch something on television, and figure out how to leave Streatham.

"Miss Berry." The abruptness with which my boss strides out of his office steals my breath, along with how—unlike me—he is unfazed. He gets as far as the door before he pauses, holds out his hand, and looks back at me.

"Is there something you need, Mr Streatham?" I venture.

Letting out an irritated huff, he drawls, "Your presence, Miss Berry."

He takes my hand and pulls me with him into the corridor.

I have no words. Who is this man, and where is my uncompromising boss? He hasn't stopped work this early since... Well. I don't think he ever has.

The Streatham headquarters is an old country mansion, with rooms off a magnificent central stairwell that curls up the middle of the house, lighted by an atrium and leading into a lobby with a patterned marble floor that is usually hushed and quiet. As we descend the stairs to the ground floor, the various other Streatham departments have open doors, and the staff are congregated. They stare at their boss, holding hands with me.

Nerves slither like snakes in my belly. Everyone is looking at us.

Mr Streatham comes to a halt at the foot of the stairs. "You got my memo, then, thank you for responding to my note."

His note? What? Mr Streatham has me write his notes to the staff.

"Today I asked Miss Berry to marry me, and I am honoured to announce that she has accepted."

There's stunned silence, then a smattering of applause that quickly turns into a roar of approval.

Oh my god. I wonder if any of them heard anything earlier...

Mr Streatham nods in acknowledgement, raises his hand like he's king, then turns to me.

"No backing out now, darling," he murmurs, catching

my wrist and bringing it up to kiss my knuckles. Heat surges through me.

He made a very public declaration that we're going to marry.

This is fine. It's fine. I'm not panicking. At all.

I'm a bit faint as, out of the corner of my eye, I can see everyone looking at me. I bet they're wondering why on earth he chose me, just his little assistant. They could be taking bets on how long it is before this blows up in my face. Probably they think this is a joke.

Mr Streatham nods again to his people, before leading me back upstairs and down the hallway, unlocking the door at the end with a hefty key.

I gasp as he leads me into what is immediately obvious is his private apartment, though it's more like a whole wing of the mansion. Where the rest of the building is dark, austere, shiny wood and stone, formal portraits and bronze statues, this is comfortable. There are bright landscape paintings, leather sofas with warm-looking throws, and richly patterned wallpaper featuring plants and birds. Predictably, there's no television, just an expensive music system and walls of books.

It feels like home.

So much so... "You have the same cushion as me!"

"I arranged for all your possessions to be delivered here and placed appropriately."

I gape up at my fiancé.

"There are a few practical items in storage that my men assumed were not of sentimental value. Although they brought the ones they thought you probably liked."

"But... How did you get into my house?" I stutter out.

Mr Streatham blinks with surprise.

"They just broke the door down," he says, as though

that's perfectly reasonable and obvious. "Your address is on file with HR," he adds because I'm staring at him, in shock for what, the fourth time today? Will I ever fully close my mouth again?

"You broke into my house?" I think I ought to be furious that he invaded my privacy? I should definitely be upset. But I'm weirdly pleased to not be managing things for once. The decision has been taken for me, every detail sorted, as though he's played at being assistant rather than a mafia boss today. Mr Streatham hasn't even asked. He's just moved me into his house.

"It was practical." He shrugs. "You were always going to move in with me, and this achieved that with no effort or fuss on your part."

I had no idea this would happen so fast, and my heart is interpreting all his haste as affection, in a loveless marriage. That's certain to get me hurt.

This breaking and entering—both to my home and my body—is insane. But he wouldn't have done this if he didn't want me, in some small way, right? Though it's far from "I love you".

There's a voice in my head and a tightness in my chest as I look at my possessions interspersed with his that says that being so close to what I truly want could be worse than only being his assistant.

Mr Streatham leads me out, still holding my hand. I follow like I'm his toy.

My eyes drag over the room he's brought me to.

His bedroom, with my "Reading is Life" sticker-covered eReader on a bedside table.

And there's one bed.

It might be huge, but the intention is very clear: I'm going to be sleeping in the same bed as my boss. The thrill that shimmers down my spine is unwarranted. This is a marriage of convenience. I mustn't read anything into his actions.

And yet...

"Now, if we're to be convincing as a couple, you need to tell me more about you, fiancée." He returns to the living room, collapses onto the sofa and appears immediately comfortable, like a lion lying down in the grass. "What was that book I caught you reading at lunchtime last week?"

I follow and prop myself up at the other end of the seat. Fingering the fluffy throw, I shake my head. "Nothing, it was just—"

"It wasn't just anything," he cuts me off. "Tell me."

So I do. I show him the romcoms with bright covers that I love to read, and his silver eyes shine when I explain the jokes—very badly. Tea and treats arrive during our conversation, like my boss-fiancé is a country gentleman.

We don't stop talking for the whole evening. About books, about family.

I should be shocked when he tells me with his customary matter-of-factness that he killed his father because he discovered he'd murdered his mother when Dex was eight. I'm not though. I'm reassured. A fifteen-year-old who cares enough about justice and revenge to do something so drastic, and then run a London mafia for twenty-four years has to be someone I can trust. Right?

And stupid as it might make me, I believe him when he says he'll read my favourite romcoms, and men who read romance have to be good, even if they're murderous kingpins. Hashtag book girly logic.

We've worked together for six months, but talking like this feels as though we're going down a path we've looked at a hundred times but never dared step onto. And now we have, it's all too natural.

I have to keep reminding myself that this is fake.

Mr Streatham narrows his eyes on my second yawn, after dinner of perfectly cooked steak and dessert that was creamy and rich.

"Bedtime," he decrees.

When I come from the shower dressed in my pyjamas, I find him already in bed, sitting up, bare chested and wearing a pair of reading glasses that turn his hot professor vibe up to fifteen bazillion and the temperature to tropical. He's reading a romcom that I recommended. One of mine, from my house, I realise.

He's silent as I shuffle across the room, struggling not to cover myself, even though the little shirt and shorts combo is far more than I wore earlier in his office. I slip under the covers, and my future husband closes his book and turns out the light.

I lie on my side, eyes open in the dark, not knowing what to do. But Mr Streatham does. He shifts and slowly runs his hands down my body, lingering at my waist. Then he sighs.

"You're tired."

I am, but I'm also electrified by his touch. I'm lit up inside, as though he's a power source and I'm a lamp.

This is an addiction. Already, I'm dangerously needy, kidding myself that he wants me too.

"I said I wanted to practise," I whisper. I crave him, even if it's a lie.

He scoops me up before I can roll over to face him, pressing me to his front, and my god. Within seconds he's pushed off my pyjamas and has me naked and gently grasps my hair, pulls my head back, and drags his bristly-but-soft beard over my shoulder.

"So sweet, and good. Fuck, I don't deserve you," he mutters, and my brain shorts out. He thinks that?

Then he's reached between my legs, and I can't get any words out because he's groaning that I'm being such a good girl for him and sliding his thick fingers into where I'm slick and hot.

I'm bracketed by him, held almost, and he strokes my clit, making me glow brighter and brighter.

He breaths in, as though relishing the scent of my hair, then pulls me closer still, his hard length pressing against my bottom.

"Let me in, little one."

Darling in public, little one in private, I vaguely note as I allow him to lift my leg. The invasion of his cock isn't so unfamiliar this time. There's a sharp pain that fades almost immediately, and then the stretch that my body already understands is the precursor to pleasure.

And then he's easing in and out of me with agonising slowness and my clit throbs as he plays with it. I'm helpless, languid and tired from an overwhelming day, and against all logic, I trust this man.

I lose all sense of time. All I can do is focus on where he's touching me, stuffing me full of him with a relentless slow rhythm. I don't know whether I'm glad of the respite when he withdraws almost to the tip, or disappointed. But eventually, I'm shaking and sobbing in his arms, and he's reassuring me with a rumble that I feel more than hear.

Then I'm falling, clutching at his solid, muscled forearms, the hair both coarse and smooth under my fingers and the pleasure sweeps from where we're joined right down to my toes in waves that surely change me at some basic level.

It's world ending.

But only for me.

Because the first thing I realise when my body is relaxed again—though sparkling with internal magic he gave me—is that he's an immovable rock in my storm.

He's still hard.

I wait, but he doesn't move. His breath is deep and even. This hasn't affected him at all?

"Do you want to..." I begin.

"What, little one?" Dex replies, subtle laughter in his tone.

I screw up my courage. "Come?"

"That's not our deal."

"No, but..." I struggle to find the way to put this thought. Surely he'd enjoy this more if he finished? That would be worthwhile, although it would reduce the chance of me getting pregnant. "Isn't it important for men?"

"Men who aren't in control of themselves, maybe."

He thrusts just enough to make me bite my lip to hold back a moan.

"Men who think they'll die from a bit of discomfort or frustration." Dex's rough voice sends a fresh shudder down my spine.

It's so weird being wrapped up in him, his arms around me, his cock lodged deep in my pussy, and not being able to see him. I'm taking all my cues from his words and his touch when usually when we talk it's face-to-face in his office. And while he's moved away from touching my clit, he's smoothing his fingers over my legs and up to my waist.

"I want to come right up here." He palms my belly. "I'll plant my seed deep inside you, and knock you up. I want to fill you until it seeps out, then force you to hold it in. I'll breed you in the morning before work and it'll slide down your inner thighs until lunchtime when I'll take you again, giving you more and more, until you're overflowing. I promise I'll give you everything you need and more to get pregnant."

Oh my god. I failed to understand. It's not going to be Dex's frustration that compromises us waiting for when I'm fertile, so I have the best chance of getting pregnant. Nope. The issue will be that I'm desperate.

Despite having had multiple orgasms today, I'm unbearably horny for *him* to be satisfied. I want to see him fall apart like I did, in the wilderness of pleasure. I need to feel his hot warm seed filling me up and know it might get me pregnant with his child.

I can't do this if I'm the only one not just in love, but hooked. Obsessed. I need his control to break and to have him desire me to the point of madness, like I do him.

I had no idea I'd be such a slut, but there you go.

Horny slut mode: engaged. Chaste little virgin: dead.

He gathers my hair up and tightens his grip. Every one of my nerve endings zings to life as he kisses and nibbles. The licks on that previously unknown sensitive spot behind my ear nearly make me come. Again.

And all the time, my pussy is stuffed with his hardness. I'm deliciously stretched.

"Men who don't understand that the greatest privilege a woman can give him is not allowing him to breed her, or pleasure him. Because that's easy… No, the best thing—the more difficult thing to achieve—is to give her overwhelming pleasure. To get her addicted to the way she feels with you."

I am definitely addicted. Already. No need for Dex to prove anything. This is a disaster.

I'm also unspeakably jealous.

"You do this for all your partners?" I ask, as casually as I can.

"Did. There's no one but you, Sophia. I'm not unfaithful. I won't do that to our child."

The baby. Right. Yes.

That's all this is.

"Should I…" I go to shift away, off him.

"No. Stay."

I blink, and try to relax.

He sighs with what sounds like contentment.

"That's it." He strokes my hair out of my eyes, and doesn't seem to notice or care that I'm a sweaty mess after orgasming multiple times. "Stay there. Go to sleep."

What?

"Yes, I said go to sleep. You said you were a virgin and needed to get used to my cock. Well. Here is your chance."

Surely I can't sleep with him inside me? Surely not?

But Dex's arms wrap around me tighter, and I relax into them. I let my muscles give way, one by one, until I'm heavy on the mattress and in his embrace.

"That's it. Sleep, little one," he rumbles into my ear.

I can't. I can't do this. My heart is trying to burst out of my body because I love him so much. How am I going to do this every night without either letting on that my feelings are so much more than his, or breaking from the pain of him not loving me back?

But despite the solid length of him still hard inside me, filling me, or perhaps because of being stuffed with cock like it's a comfort, I fall asleep. Fear and all.

I try to forget the heartbreak ahead.

9

SOPHIA

I wake up wrapped in the best blanket. Warm, comforting, deliciously male. I'm lying on my side, and he's pressed up behind me, our legs entwined.

My fiancé.

It all returns in a rush. I'm going to be married to my boss, and we're in his bed together. He took my virginity and promised to marry me and give me his baby. Mr Streatham said I was his good girl.

I shift experimentally, and something solid touches my bottom.

"Mmm." Behind me, Mr Streatham gives a rumbling purr. "Sore?" he asks.

"No." And the word is hardly out of my mouth, but he's got me bent at the waist, revealing where I'm wet and needy.

"Is this what you want, little one?" The hot, silken tip of his cock nudges against my thigh. "Breeding practice?"

No, I want his love. I wish this was a real engagement, but that's delusional.

"Yes," I whisper, trying to wiggle to get him inside me.

Because if I can't have his love, then this is an acceptable second.

"Let's try it this way," he murmurs and flips me so I'm on my front, underneath him in one fluid movement. His knees push between mine, and he's feeding that massive thing into me, inch by glorious inch.

It's easier this time. My body knows his, and I breathe through the sting.

He pauses at the hilt. Then he starts to move.

Oh my god.

If I ever thought Mr Streatham was big, I had no idea. Because above me and inside me, he's enormous. He's overwhelming.

I'm entirely at his mercy, trapped, being pushed into the mattress with every push of him into me. He's infuriatingly slow, as though he has forever to get all the way into me with that long, thick cock.

But he's effective. So, very thorough, that I come even more easily this time. Once. And then again, holding my face into the pillow as I scream and shudder.

"My god, Sophia." He gives a low chuckle when I turn my head and try to see him, my orgasm dying away. "The things you do to me..."

He slides out of me with a wet pop, and I'm immediately bereft. Empty, or rather, even more empty.

"Not make you come," I mutter.

"Not yet, darling," he says lightly, pushing off the covers.

Something dark and prickly twists in my chest. I didn't anticipate this being frustrating. Surely it shouldn't matter whether he finds release? I'm getting a higher chance of becoming pregnant. That should be enough, and yet I'm left feeling more and more denied every time Mr Streatham doesn't climax.

I cast a sideways look at his erection. It's glistening with my juices, and he's in control. It's ridiculous, but I want him to come more than I want another orgasm myself. I wish he was as affected by this relationship as I am.

Honestly, I'm chasing the impossible: for my severe boss to love me.

He rolls out of bed, and I peek at his gloriously naked body. He's beautiful. He might be older than me and nearly forty, but he's trim and muscular. I've never seen a man in real life, naked, not close to. And certainly not nude and aroused. I'm entranced. His cock from this angle is a thing of beauty, long, proudly jutting up, smooth. My mouth waters.

I will never get used to seeing him like this, not in a month of Mondays…

It's only then that I realise it's a weekday and I have no idea what the time is. "Mr Streatham?"

"Dex." He turns and regards me, hands on his tie. "You should call me Dex since you're going to be my wife."

There's an emphasis on those last two words that sizzles across my skin. His wife.

"Dex." His name is illicit and powerful on my tongue. "What about work?"

"We're taking the day off to get married."

Up until yesterday, I thought I was unshockable. I'm the private assistant to a mobster, after all. I've seen Mr Streatham covered in blood. I've seen people coming in for meetings and never leaving. I've booked drug raids into his schedule and typed up notes from interrogations.

My disciplined boss is taking the day off?

"What about Operation Calculus?"

"It can wait." He finishes his tie with practised hands, and I can't keep my eyes off him.

"But—"

"Everything can wait, today, Sophia. Everything, except getting married."

Oh wow. He's serious about this.

"Isn't it bad luck for the groom to see the bride before the wedding?" The last thing I need is bad luck, and my boss is conventional. I'm surprised he hasn't thought of this.

Mr Streatham sighs like I'm being very tedious. "That's a superstition left over from arranged marriages—"

"Which ours is—" I point out.

"When the groom seeing the bride beforehand risked him deeming her not attractive enough, and not going through with the marriage."

Oh.

I don't know what to say to that.

"I won't change my mind, little one."

"You won't?" There's a tremor of uncertainty in my voice.

"No." And when I look up at him, he's as serious as I've ever seen him. "Not least because you're very pretty."

That comment settles onto my chest like spring blossom. "Thank you," I murmur.

He shakes his head dismissively.

"It's only, this is really quick…" I say, mostly to myself. That's what I wanted, isn't it? It doesn't matter that he doesn't love me. I was never going to have love from my husband, only maybe, my children.

"There's a Maths Club meeting later this week," he replies. "I want to introduce you as my wife."

Right. Yes.

And as I get up and dressed, thankful that Mr

Streatham leaves me alone to do so with a curt, "I'll be back," I keep that in mind. The only reason we're doing this is so I have a child, and Dex has a wife.

Being reminded he doesn't actually want *me* makes me shy about what I've been doing. Basically, I threw myself at my boss. I'm glad I don't have to dress in front of him. He's seen me with no clothes on, but there's horny nude, and then there's "which of these knickers is least grey" naked. I am not convinced I'm attractive in either scenario, but I don't want my boss watching me wiggling into my jeans.

I'm particularly glad for white underwear when he takes me dress shopping after an extravagant breakfast. I try on the first dress then hesitate at the curtain leading out of the changing room.

He said he was going to help me choose a dress because otherwise I'd be alone, but I'm still irrationally worried about giving us bad luck. What if I don't get pregnant because of him seeing the dress before the wedding?

But then, if I can't get pregnant within six months, will Dex be one of those people who used to be close to me, and then forgot? The fair-weather friends who wanted to hang out with me when it was convenient but didn't bother to keep in touch when school, university, or our jobs took us in different directions. Who never phones or messages?

I guess he wouldn't, since I don't think he even owns a smartphone.

"Come out here," Dex calls from the main part of the shop.

I don't respond, because I think my voice would emerge with all the melodic grace of a five-year-old playing the violin.

Oh shit, Sophia, don't cry. Do. Not. Cry.

I exhale. Perhaps I don't need luck, or already have it. Because despite all the odds, I'm marrying my boss.

Drawing back the curtain, I see Dexter lounged on a sofa, knees arrogantly sprawled apart. His neck shifts as he swallows, and unbidden, excitement curls in me. This man is gorgeous.

"No. Not that one," he states immediately.

"But it's good, isn't it? Demure." I indicate the high neckline. I thought this would be what he'd like.

His eyebrows pinch together. "Mmm. Try something more revealing."

The next dress is outrageous. Low cut and sparkling with diamantes. Dex drags his gaze down my body in a lingering way that leaves no room for ambiguity. I squirm.

"It's sexy," he says. "And you look beautiful, but it's not the right one."

We go through a dozen dresses, all equally gorgeous. Each dress I show to my fiancé he compliments me, says that I look lovely, but shakes his head.

Then there's a dress that's silky inside, and has just the right neckline. When I catch sight of the girl in the mirror in the changing room, she isn't dull or boring... She's... Beautiful.

Bouncing onto tiptoes, I know. This. This is a dress that feels worthy of a groom like the Streatham kingpin.

I almost run out to show Dex, sweeping back the curtain and rushing until he glances up from writing notes and I realise too late I was trying to be dignified.

"That's the one," he says instantly. He nods, not even looking at the dress, his gaze remaining on my face.

"You've seen it for all of a second," I laugh, sheer surprise bubbling through me. I thought I'd have to persuade him. "Why this dress?"

Dex studies my face.

The energy between us rises and the closeness is so odd. I've had sex with this man, and spent whole days working with him. I slept with him inside me. We woke up together.

But it's only now that I have the bone-deep sensation that he knows me, as he sees me in this perfect dress.

"Because of that smile," he says in a low, hoarse voice that gives shivers down my spine to heat between my legs. "I know it's the right dress for you because of your face when you came out wearing it."

He likes it because it made me happy? Is that the nicest thing anyone has ever said to me?

The rest of the day is a blur. Once I'm back in my jeans shorts and top, the dress arranged to be altered and delivered, Dex takes my hand and guides me out of the door. I go with no fuss. I'm along for the ride in my own life for maybe the first time ever. I'm not arranging anything, or doing the work.

I kind of like it. My husband is in control.

The next stop is a jeweller, and Dex is intent on playing the attentive fiancé there, too. He slips a casual arm around my waist as we walk away from the car and into the shop, and my brain stutters at how protective and possessive it feels to have his enormous body beside mine, and his big hand warm on me.

Just like with the dresses, Dex watches over me as I try on different metals and designs, and we eventually settle on matching yellow-gold bands and a huge diamond engagement ring for me. My fake fiancé pockets the wedding bands, and takes my hand without fanfare, sliding the engagement ring on.

The band is heavy, and feels like a lock of ownership snapping shut. It's an echo of when he penetrated me yesterday.

Back at the Streatham mansion, Dex takes me to his apartment, which is a buzz of activity. A hair stylist, the assistant from the bridal shop, a makeup artist, and a photographer all introduce themselves and I'm so swept up in wedding preparations that initially I don't notice that my husband-to-be has disappeared.

And it's only when I'm instructed to wait a moment when everything is ready that I realise something is wrong. Very wrong.

I push free and peek outside, and the problem is immediately obvious.

There's an archway decorated with dusky pink roses, and Streatham Common stretching out beyond. An officiant waits patiently and seated on either side of an aisle are the Streatham employees I've worked with. Bulky enforcers, assistants like me, house staff, and dozens of contacts I've dealt with in the past six months. Our people, I realise. Or they will be mine too, once I'm the kingpin of Streatham's wife.

But Mr Streatham *isn't there*.

He's jilting me.

The humiliation isn't hot and sweet like being embarrassed yesterday was. No, this is a cold, creeping sensation. Every uncertainty rises and surrounds me like a swarm of insects I've been batting from my face for the last day.

Dex isn't there.

I cannot do this.

My first instinct was right. I want to help Mr Streatham,

but I'd be crazy to tie myself forever to having children with a man who won't love me. I head blindly away from the door, heading for the stairs to get out of this dress and run. Somewhere, anywhere.

"Miss Berry."

I stop, instinctively obedient to Mr Streatham's harsh voice.

"Where are you going?"

Excuses scroll through my mind. I forgot my phone? No. I need to water the flowers in this bouquet. I thought I might run away to Australia after all. I'm actually a were-wolf and the full moon is rising. Lost your chance of a human bride by being late, bad luck. Shouldn't have seen the dress.

"Nowhere." But I don't move.

"Darling," he says more softly, from right behind me.

My heart thumps. The unfamiliar weight of the dress puts me off-balance as I turn to Dex. On the first step of the stairs, I'm only a bit shorter than my boss. He's wearing a dark suit, and immediately I see is a spec of blood. Fear surges in me.

"I'm sorry I'm late, darling. There was an Essex Cartel incident," he says calmly.

I reach for his lapel, covering the mark.

Whatever delayed him, and it was only a moment, must have been important. Was I really going to run away? When he says he needs me?

He slowly places his hand over mine. I'm too shy to look at him, but it's like my soul is reaching out, pushing through my skin, the silk, the air, his shirt, and trying to link to him. I think we're closer than we've ever been before, with or without clothes on.

Maybe it's the gravity of the situation. We're going to be married.

"Sophia," he breathes.

I try to let my hand fall away, but he moves with me, interlocking our fingers so they're joined at our waists.

"Dex, are we doing the right thing?" I ask in a whisper, giving voice to the surface of my fears. This is a marriage of convenience for me to have babies and him to gain influence. Of course it's the wrong thing for me, because I've already broken the unwritten rule: don't fall in love.

"I am." His voice is a smooth and confident bass. "Why are you concerned?"

"You're a billionaire kingpin, and my boss, and I'm just... Me." A girl who is so out of her depth she's doing splashy doggy-paddle to stay afloat.

"Ahh. I understand." He tightens his grip on my hand, and for a second, I think perhaps he really does. "I'll never cheat on you. I swear on my life and yours, and that of the baby I'm going to give you."

It's not that, although obviously his oath helps.

It's that I'm in love with him, and he'll never know.

"Now, are we getting married?"

"Yes." Because scared as I am of being hurt, opportunities to marry your silver-fox crush only happen once in a lifetime. However painful anything that happens next might be, surely it's better than not having him at all.

"Good." Then he adds under his breath, "Because I wouldn't have let you go." But it's so soft, as our gazes meet, I think I imagined it, because that hardness has dissipated from his titanium eyes.

Even so, my tummy is full of butterflies as Dex leaves me at the door to the house and stands waiting, a lone figure beneath the arch of flowers. Music swells as I walk towards him and he watches every step I take, gaze so intent and hungry I almost stumble.

The sun is low on the horizon, the sky stained pink-purple. He takes my hand again and something settles in my chest. This is where I'm supposed to be.

A pair of birds wheel high above us, and the air is fragrant with lavender and roses as we exchange our vows. To love and honour. To cherish. To love. I choke up a bit as I speak that word, and Dex squeezes my fingers reassuringly. It's all elegant and low-key and intimate.

Okay, it's gorgeously romantic.

Fine. Heartbreakingly romantic for a marriage of convenience, made all the more meaningful because Dex arranged it.

And I'm an idiot. Because when I look up into my husband's face after the officiant announces, "You may kiss the bride", I have rose-tinted glasses on. His colourless eyes seem pink in the setting sun.

It's fake.

But despite me knowing that this is a pretence, I'm swooning.

There's a click from a camera.

"Family photos," Dex murmurs. "For our kids. Better look like we're the loving parents they deserve." Then he pushes my chin back around towards him and tilts my face to receive his kiss.

It's sweet and rough from his beard, and any reservations I had fade. The camera clicks again, and I shut my eyes and focus on him. My husband. The scary mafia boss who planned our wedding, right down to a photographer and insisting on finding not just a lovely dress, but the *perfect* one.

And when his mouth touches mine, I know for certain I cannot live without this man. Six months isn't enough.

Whatever the cost, I must get pregnant.

10

DEX

Our wedding night is torture.

Well, for me it is. Sophia seems to enjoy it. I make her come multiple times, and she takes my cock in almost every way except for me on top of her. I don't think I have the self-restraint to have her beneath me, all wet and pliant and hazy eyed from orgasm, and not blow my load.

I have control, but I'm not a man without appetites.

I manage to tire her out enough that she doesn't wake, and we remain joined like that, her body a perfectly fitting sheath.

The days crawl by.

I circle the date in my agenda, and tick off the days that pass like I'm a prisoner. But instead of being held by the Camden mafia and my blood flowing, the issue is the lack of outlets for bodily fluids.

Ten, nine, eight.

The time until Sophia will be fertile feels to be getting longer, not shorter.

Seven, six.

I can't concentrate.

I fuck up a message to the Tiptree, the Essex kingpin I'm arranging to enact a coup with, and only just prevent the whole plan from being sent to our enemies. Sophia catches my mistake, clever creature that she is. She's blooming, but there's a shadow behind her eyes when she thinks I'm not looking. It bothers me that there's something she's sad about, and that she's hiding it from me.

I do what I can to please her. I spoil her with new books. I use the excuse of teaching her about sex to fuck her slow and thoroughly with her on top in the evening, use her pussy to keep my cock warm overnight, and have her from behind in the morning.

I've edged myself so hard over the days since our bargain that I'm constantly in danger of falling over. After six months of nothing but Sophia's face in my imagination as I paint my hand or the shower white when I've longed for her, the change to having *my wife* whenever I want, but being unable to release is sheer irony.

Five, four.

Being married helps, to an extent. I shamelessly use the excuse of making our relationship seem genuine to kiss her, hold her close, and generally be much more handsy than a man sixteen years older than her should be.

I said I'd endure anything to have her, and I will. I just didn't realise it would be so *hard*.

But it'll be worthwhile, I tell myself as my cock attempts to spring up—again—whenever I look at Sophia.

There are still three twenty-nine-thousand-hour days until I can claim my wife fully. But at least this evening I have the ideal excuse for pretending to be as pathetically in love as I really am.

"Do they know you're married?" Sophia asks,

smoothing down her dress as we enter the hotel where the London Maths Club are having a social dinner event.

"Yes." I put an announcement of our marriage in *The Times*, *The Evening Standard*, and all the local newspapers too, as well as having some of the most flattering candid shots from the wedding leaked to the gossip magazines. I assume it will have filtered through to Snap Tick Book or whatever online thing is fashionable now.

"Right. Good. That's good." She takes a deep breath. "What if they don't like me?"

"Then I'll kill them." Her hand is so small in mine.

"Dex!" she chides, but there's laughter in her voice. "Gaining the approval of these people is the reason you married me. Murder isn't going to achieve that."

"If anyone disrespects you in the slightest, they'll be fertilising the roses on Streatham Common," I mutter, and I'm saved from responding to Sophia about what I mean by a deferential young man taking our coats. Bone meal and blood are excellent for roses, and Streatham has won best-kept part of London since my grandfather's time. My father even contributed *personally*.

At the entrance to the private dining room, I pause and tighten my grip on Sophia's hand. We're only a few minutes late, but everyone is already sitting around a long table set with pristine white cloths and tableware.

Westminster notices us first, almost immediately, as he does nearly everything going on in the London Mafia Syndicate. He stands up, smirks, and claps. Within seconds they're all on their feet, smiling and offering congratulations.

"Fuck's sake, not another marriage," grumbles Richmond. "It's like bloody Vegas around here."

The fury is fast and hot. Sophia is nothing so crass as a

Vegas bride, and I'm about to put him right when there's a tug from Sophia on my arm. When I look down at her, she has that "What are you doing?" expression. It's cool water over my temper.

None of this matters. Only her.

"This is my wife, Sophia Streatham." I love the ownership that has her name paired with mine. "Darling, this is the London Mafia Syndicate."

There are nods and hellos, and a dizzying array of introductions and we take our seats between Westminster and Canary Wharf. I've never much cared for the way couples are seated beside each other with the men and women paired, but I see the sense of it now. It means there isn't a man next to my wife, and I can relax a bit.

"I'm so glad you two have a love match!" The wife of the Canary Wharf kingpin, Adi Cavendish, beams at Sophia. I think only I would recognise that Sophia's returned smile is underlaid with horror.

Because it's not a love match, is it? Sophia thinks we're fooling them all for my sake. When in fact, I'm pretending to love her, whilst pretending not to love her, and using them as an excuse.

A complete mess.

"Do you like to read?" Adi asks with a smile once the food is being served and the worst of the small talk is done. "You're welcome to join the London Maths Club, also known as our little reading group?"

"Oh, there's a book club?" Sophia pauses.

"Look, this is a problem," Lina leans across the table, and says in a tone that suggests this is not the first time she's made this point, "It's the London Mafia Smut Club. No one will join if they think it has to do with maths."

"Maths isn't that bad," Cassie, who is one of the Blackwood triplets' wives, interjects from the other end of the table.

"Clearly we're doing fine for recruitment, because Sophia is going to join," Adi replies.

Lina rolls her eyes. "You're just protecting your husband—"

"So, there's no maths club?" Sophia asks.

Westminster and Mayfair share a look.

Canary Wharf folds his arms. "I'm not taking responsibility for the continued shitshow about the maths club."

"What is the London Maths Club?" Sophia asks quietly.

And honestly, I'm glad she's asked, because I've never inquired why a mafia syndicate loves maths-themed jokes.

"It stands for Mobsters And Thugs Hate Spaghetti," says Angel, straight-faced.

"Hey!" Marco Brent bangs the table. "I love spaghetti."

Jessa smirks. "The Maths Club refers to the obsession of this lot with comparing the size of their *magic numbers*..."

"Nothing wrong with a large... Number of kills," adds her husband, Grant Lambeth.

"One of the babies had a lisp," says Anwyn, Westminster's wife, blinking innocently. "Couldn't say mafia and it caught on."

Mayfair folds his arms, sighing. "Just an innocent misunderstanding. Right."

"My husband thought I didn't know he was a mafia boss." Adi smiles and looks up nostalgically. "He accidentally started to say Mafia Syndicate, got halfway through, and 'Maths Club' was the best he came up with. Everyone played along. It was hilarious."

"Don't be silly, no one would believe that." Canary Wharf has a glint in his eyes as he pulls his wife in for a kiss.

"You know, it could refer to the precision of the Syndicate's work and our adherence to balancing the equation of justice," Westminster says thoughtfully.

There's a pause when everyone looks at the best-known face of the London mafias.

"That really is ridiculous," Mayfair drawls, his Russian accent coming out.

"Fine." Westminster shakes his head. "We're the Mobsters And Thugs who Hate Spinach though, not spaghetti. Italian food is well loved around here."

"I wouldn't have made it through any of my pregnancies without pizza and spaghetti," agrees Jessa, exchanging nods with Anwyn.

The conversation diverges to babies, and Sophia listens, eyes sparkling, to the other women's tales of their children's births.

Soon, I promise her. *That will be us, very soon, little one.*

"How is Operation Calculus going?" Westminster asks from across the table. "I'm still not sure we can trust Tiptree."

"We can." I level a look at the kingpin who thinks he runs London. He doesn't know what he doesn't know. "Tiptree is not the problem." I'm still not certain I did the right thing letting them live, but Sophia doesn't like too much death. Thank god she doesn't know about the man I dispatched on our wedding day. "I think he's okay, but that doesn't mean we haven't got problems elsewhere."

Over the next few hours, my body is a combat zone between pride in my wife making friends with the mafia wives and the instinct to take her home and have the relief and agony of her on my cock and under my mouth. Dessert is particularly taxing, as Sophia decadently licks her poached peach and raspberries with whipped cream.

Cream. Whole mouthfuls of it. Is my girl trying to kill me from lack of blood supply to any organ other than my cock?

"They seem nice," Sophia comments as we eventually arrive home. "Not cliquey in the way you suggested. Was it better being married?"

And there's only one possible answer. I breathe in the fragrant night air and help her out of the car, utterly focused on Sophia. None of my mafia work matters by comparison.

She's the axis upon which my world spins.

"Yes. It was easier with you." I draw her to me, and whisper in her ear. "Everything is better now that you're mine."

Our gazes meet and confusion shadows her pretty, speckled eyes.

"Because I'm your wife, you mean?"

She's so much more than that. She's my obsession, my life, my darling. She's the only reason I have any internal organs or feelings. She's the start of everything, and the longing to see her swollen with my baby is an almost unbearable ache in my chest.

My sweet, good girl. I need to get inside her. I drag in a breath, and, her hand in mine, guide her towards Streatham House.

The only way I can truly feel at peace is when she's coming, that's the truth.

There's a glint of silver from the side, and I act on instinct.

I throw myself over Sophia, falling to the ground and not even able to turn us in time so I cushion her fall.

A bullet yanks me aside, away from her, and pain tears through me. Then it's black.

11

SOPHIA

"Dex!" The cry is out of my throat as panic surges through me. I'm vaguely aware of a screech of tyres, the thud of feet, and a hard smack of something on my thigh, but Dex has been propelled off me. My heart in my mouth.

I throw myself up and a sob rises as I see him. His eyes are closed, he's on his back.

He can't be dead, he *can't* be.

"Dex!" I grip his lapels. His black tuxedo hides everything and for a second the shimmering over my eyes and the yellow light convince me there's blood everywhere.

"Mrs Streatham." The voice of one of the Streatham men comes from behind me.

Then Dex's eyes snap open. "Sophia. Are you alright?"

The relief makes me lightheaded as Dex grabs my shoulders and scans my face and body. "Darling. Are you hurt?"

"No, but—"

"Boss, your arm..." His man says tentatively.

"What?" I yank back, and for once Dex doesn't hold me.

Immediately I see why. There's a tear in his tux at his upper arm.

Dex groans and winces as he pushes up to a sitting position. "Fuckers."

I'm suddenly aware that I'm kneeling on the prickly tarmac. We both are.

"We have to get inside." I try to help him up and he lets out a tired laugh. "What if they're still—"

"They've gone. Didn't hang around," the Streatham man says as Dex rises to his feet.

Dex pulls me into his arms, even as I protest about the actual bullet wound that he needs to deal with. "It's okay," he murmurs, turning us towards the house.

"What...? Oh shit..."

He stops abruptly, looking at my legs. For a split-second I think I'm injured and with all the adrenaline I don't realise.

"Poor Tiptree." Dex's expression goes dark.

I follow his gaze. On the ground beside us is a severed human head. I jerk in fright, and Dex grips my waist harder with one hand.

It's a man in his sixties, or maybe even older. His eyes are closed, and his pale blond and silver hair is sticking up at all angles. Bile jumps up my throat. I recognise that face. He came to the office once, and I took messages for him. Brian Tiptree.

And he's dead. Brutally murdered by the Essex cartel because he tried to work with the London Mafia Syndicate.

"Inside," Dex says in a tone that brooks no argument. "Now."

He doesn't let go of me once we're in the house, and I don't release his hand either. I hold it stupidly tight as the

Streatham doctor cuts Dex's shirt and jacket off him, and tends to his wound.

I play the whole event through my mind as Dex demands answers about how the Essex Cartel got through his security.

Dex is hurt. Either one of us could have been killed. He instinctively flattened me to the floor to save me, and was shot in the process.

I've never worried about working for a mafia boss. In fact, I've felt safer with Dex than at any other time. But as the doctor cleans and stitches up Dex's bullet wound, it's impressed on me that life is precious.

Life is short.

We've been messing around, waiting for me to be at peak fertility before he comes inside me, and it might have never even had the smallest chance. An aim a few inches lower, or if Dex hadn't reacted as quickly as he did... We could both be dead, or worse still, he'd have died to save me, and left me alone again. Without the man I need most in the world, or even his baby to comfort me in my grief.

He would have died never knowing that I love him with all my heart. Or I could have taken my secret feelings to the grave.

"Go to bed," Dex says when the bleeding has mainly stopped. "Get some sleep. I need to find whoever did this, so don't wait up."

"No." I'm aware that it was partly my fault that this happened. Dex wanted to kill the men he suspected of treachery, and I convinced him not to. "When you're injured is not the right time. You don't even know who it was. You could be going up against the whole Essex Cartel." And that would be suicide, even for a London mafia boss as powerful and connected as Streatham.

"You've just been shot, Boss," the doctor chides gently. "Your wife has a point."

Dex swallows, his mouth set in a furious line.

"They could have fired again," one of the Streatham men adds. "If it had been me, and I'd been trying to kill anyone, I would have given it a go. Are we sure it was a full assassination attempt?"

"Streatham and the London Maths Club have been attempting to defang the Essex Cartel with a coup," I say. "They might just want us to back off."

Dex pauses, his brows low as he considers. "This was mainly a warning. We'll accept it as such. For now."

He orders a double guard watch and then leads me to his quarters with a bleak, stony look in his eyes that scares me almost as much as the shooting.

Locking the door behind us, Dex releases my hand, and I'm left standing in his home where all our possessions are mixed in together.

"Do you want to leave?" Dex asks abruptly.

"What?" I stare at my husband.

"I wouldn't blame you." His gaze skates away to the empty fireplace. "I should have protected you."

"Dex, you did!" He literally threw himself over me and got shot to keep me from harm.

"I should have anticipated this. I swore you'd be safe as my wife." He sighs and shakes his head. "You deserve better."

My heart cracks. "Are you trying to get rid of me?"

He looks at his bandaged arm and his jaw clenches.

"We have a bet." Life is short, I remind myself. "I'm not leaving, and you're going to give me a *baby*."

He scowls. "In two days, and then—"

"No." The word is squeaky.

He goes still.

"I need you to come inside me. You're not going after the Essex Cartel, and you're not dying. You could have *died*, Dex." Emotion wells up from my feet, flooding up to my chest, then higher, threatening to drown me. "Give me a baby *now*."

"Hey, hey, little one," he croons and pulls me into his arms. "There's no need to cry. You'd be a very wealthy widow if anything happened."

A watery sob fights with a fire of frustration. Why can't he understand? "But I wouldn't have *you*."

"Would that matter?" he asks wryly, and his eyebrows twitch down as he takes in my expression of furious horror. "Oh, because you wanted a father for your child, right."

"No, you idiot! No!" The stupid bargain. I can't take this any longer. "It would matter because—"

"Hey, it's alright." He's soothing me as though I'm the one who's hurt.

"Because I love you!"

12

DEX

I don't know who is most shocked by Sophia's outburst. We stare at each other for an amount of time that could be seconds, or long enough to fly to the moon.

She *loves* me?

Sophia, my darling girl, loves *me*?

Maybe I move first, or perhaps she does, but that doesn't matter because she's in my arms and I'm kissing her and she's kissing me. My cock hardens and thickens, turning to rock in the moment it takes me to back her against the wall and press myself to her.

So she can't leave.

"I love you too," I say between kisses, holding her so tight I'd risk cracking her ribs if the searing pain from my arm didn't prevent me from getting her even closer. "I love you so—"

"Dex, you don't have to—" she says, clinging to my shoulders and trying to kiss my cheek as I bury my face in her shoulder and kiss her neck ferociously.

"I do." I'm grasping at her clothes like I'm a desperate animal, ravenous to kiss her and touch her and tell her all the things in my heart simultaneously. "I've loved you from the beginning."

"No, I know it's just because of the London Maths—"

"No."

"But—"

"Okay, wait-wait-wait." I force myself to stop pawing her and pulling her nearer. She whimpers as I cup her face, draw back, and gaze into her eyes. "Look at me."

I'm lost for a second in her mossy eyes, the pattern of gold and brown and green. There's vulnerability and worry there that I've never seen so clearly before.

"I proposed marriage because I wanted *you*."

Her breath hitches. "Really?"

Brushing my thumb over the drying tears, I nod. "It was never anything less than real, to me."

"Me neither," she says, a smile lighting her face. "That list described the only man I've ever wanted: you."

I lean my forehead on hers and close my eyes. I cannot believe this.

"My darling, my little one. I love you so much." It's a relief to tell her this and feel her nod in agreement. "You make me real. Almost forty years, and I've never felt this way. Before you, my life was a question I couldn't answer, and then you appeared, and it clicked. I knew that I'd never want anyone else. I can't breathe without you."

For a few seconds, there's just the peace of having her close, and knowing we're both in love. My heart expands big enough to envelop her and half the city.

"No more bet. That was only to ensure you had no reason not to marry me. I'm in love with you, and you're mine." My voice is gravelly. "Whatever happens next, whether you're pregnant or not, you're *my wife*. Forever. I could never have let you go."

She giggles. "I think I'd have had to resort to stuffing a pillow up top if I hadn't been pregnant after six months."

"I'd have gone along with it." I run my hands up the curve of her back. "And I'll still give you a baby, I swear."

"But no more waiting." She reaches for my belt, and I groan. "Enough restraint. I want you to come inside me."

"With pleasure." And then we're undressing each other, hands clashing, arms tangling, and I try to kiss her at the same time. I can't get her close enough.

I consider the wall as the quickest place to breed her, but I do have a tiny part of me that's still sane, so grab Sophia to me and drag her to our room and to the bed.

"Dex! Your arm! Be careful of your arm!"

I ignore her protest, and set her down, immediately covering her body with mine. It hurts, but I don't care. I need her more.

"Get your clothes off quickly, before I rip them off." She's wearing too much, having focused on pushing off my tuxedo jacket.

Yanking off my tie, I lift my shirt over my head and shove down my trousers. Both of our shoes were lost somewhere over by the bedroom door.

She's scrabbling at her back. "Help me with this zip?"

Rolling onto her side, she sweeps her hair away from the back of her neck and exposes a barely visible seam.

"This is a fussy dress," I grumble as my big fingers fail to grip the tiny button at the top.

"It doesn't matter. Just get it off."

"Do you mean that?"

"Yes—"

Whatever else she was going to say is drowned out by the sound of silk ripping. There's no finesse as I grab handfuls of the fabric and tear until I can see her skin, and push the ruined garment off her shoulders.

"Sophia, fuck," I breathe as the silk reveals that she's bare between the legs, and has no bra on either. "Don't move, little one."

My cock springs up as I rid myself of the last of my clothes, so we're both naked. Sophia drags off her dress fully and rolls over onto her back. It's a caress as she looks down my body.

"I told you to stay still." I brace myself over her and my swollen cock, a vein standing out, pulsing, and the head almost purple, slides over her belly.

"I couldn't." She pushes her hips up and spreads her legs as I settle on top of her. "Please. I need you."

"Brat."

Her hand slides between us and finds my cock, encircling the sensitive head and I hiss as pleasure flares out from where we touch. My control is hanging by a thread.

"Sophia," I choke. "If you can't be trusted to behave, I will be forced to make you, given I'm injured." I probably could stay sane with most of what has happened tonight, but with my protective instinct triggered, I'm delving into craziness. It's the pain and shock of nearly losing Sophia.

And most of all, it's that she *loves* me.

"But I want to touch you," she complains.

Her other hand sneaks down and finds my balls and cups them, the sensation elevating the caress of her fingers around my cock.

"I won't last, darling." I grit out the warning.

"I don't care."

"You will if you make come right here, over your belly, and you don't get pregnant."

She writhes, circling her hips. This girl is all innocent sexuality and I'm weak in the face of it.

"You could push it into me. Rub it into my skin."

"Stop being a brat," I say harshly.

She pouts. "Make me."

It's the matter of a second to clutch both her hands in one of mine and snatch up my tie.

"Dex!" She looks up at me with wide eyes.

"I told you to behave, given I was injured," I say severely. "So are you going to be a good girl, or will I have to tie up my brat and breed her?"

The way she licks her lips and squirms, offering up those sweet tits, tells me her answer.

I lean down and kiss her as I ruthlessly pin her hands.

"I will take you, and breed you, little one," I promise as I wrap the silk. She doesn't fight me, but she does test her bonds as I secure her wrists to the headboard.

It's the work of only a few moments, and then I draw back, and she's perfectly exposed for me. So beautiful, and in my power.

"Tempting though it is to tease you…" I mutter, covering her with my body again. Slight and tiny compared to me, I feel big and brutish, and my cock likes that she's small and trapped.

I touch the crown of my cock to where she's hot and soft and needy.

"So wet. You want this, don't you?"

A keening sound is all the reply I get as I press into her slowly. She's so tight, she feels amazing.

"Tell me again that you love me." My voice is hoarse as I kiss her mouth, only letting up to allow her to speak the words I'll never be tired of hearing.

"I love you."

"I love you too, little one." I sink into her, one slow, blissful inch at a time, deeper and deeper, until we're fully joined, as close as we can be, chest to chest and hip to hip. I grind against her, and she gasps. "I love you more than you'll ever know."

Looking into her eyes, I'm lost. My brain is incapable of taking in the way she's so perfect, and she's mine.

This was absolutely worth being shot for.

The first slide out and sink back in deep tears a moan from both of us, then I do it again, faster, harder, and before I know it the pleasure is making me crazy. "Oh fuck, I love having you in my power. You wanted me to lose control?" I tell her as I thrust into her. I roughly palm her breast and squeeze, swiping my thumb across the nipple. "This is it. This is your monster."

And instead of being scared, Sophia moans and replies, "Yes. Mine. *My* monster."

When she tilts her hips and tries to get me deeper, I can't deal with it. I can't control myself for this special moment, and keep her in check too.

"Sophia." I grab her waist and hold her down. "You're going to make me come before…"

I let out a sound like a wounded animal as she squeezes her pussy around my cock.

"Come inside me," she urges. "Fill me up."

"Not before you do," I grunt, my brain almost entirely sawing in and out of my wife.

But she's unstoppable. I cram my hand between us and find her clit. Then I summon all my strength and watch her disbelief as I stroke her in sync with my thrusts into her willing body. She tightens around my length as I get my thumb right in the best spot, then it doesn't take much. She's screaming and shuddering as she comes apart. And fuck, it's so good to feel and see her come, it nearly tips me over.

"Good girl, good girl. That's it. You did well," I tell her as the pulsing of her orgasm recedes. I kiss her cheeks and give her shallow, slow thrusts that prolong her ecstasy. "You came. Now you're going to take everything I give you."

"Dex. Husband." She wraps her legs around my waist eagerly as I accelerate and fuck her deeper. "I love you. Make me yours forever."

So I grab her thigh and push it up, opening her wider, and ram into her, the pleasure escalating immediately.

"You wanted me feral," I tell her, hoarse with need. "This is your wish."

"Yes. Breed me. I'm yours."

Then I really lose control.

13

SOPHIA

I thought I knew about sex, having experienced it with Dex before.

But, no. I was as good as a virgin, because this isn't the same act at all. This is Dex off-leash. He's ferocious. He's taking and giving, even as I'm melted butter from coming. His mouth is on my breasts, biting and licking as he pounds into me.

It's all I can do to take it.

With my hands tied, I can't explore his body or do anything but be overwhelmed by how much he needs me. I hadn't realised how he held back as he made me orgasm over and over again during the past few days, but it's clear now. Dex is giving me everything, and it's rough and animalistic and I love it.

He sucks my nipple without mercy, and I arch. My hands are tightly restrained by his tie, and not being able to move heightens the eroticism of this whole act. Like I really am just his to breed and use as he likes.

But instead of the selfishness that implies, he's still intent on me. The way he worships my breasts as he fucks me zings pleasure to my core. He's taking what he wants from my pussy and giving to me by worshipping my nipples. And between kisses and licks, his words are filthy and the sort of adoration I never dreamed a girl like me could inspire.

"I'm never letting you go, Sophia. I love you so much I want to be constantly inside you. In your body, in your head. I want to be in your every thought and have you with me. *My wife.*"

He's pounding me into the mattress. It's all I can do to dig my heels into his buttocks and keep angling my hips.

One such shift, and he groans like I'm killing him, and hits deeper, right up against my cervix.

"Fuck, you're being such a good girl taking my cock. My perfect little brat."

"Breed me, Dex. Give me a baby," I whisper back. "I'll be your good girl, I promise." Even if being a brat has turned out even better than I could have dared dream.

"However long it takes, little one, I'm not letting you go. You're mine now. No other man will ever touch you."

That sounds great to me.

"I love you. I'm obsessed, and have been since we met. I can't breathe without you."

The things this man says are short-circuiting my brain.

"My love, my darling, my obsession, my wife, my little one." He punctuates each word with a kiss, peppering them sweetly over my face as he slams into my pussy. "I can't believe you're finally *mine* in every way. You're going to have my baby, and I'm going to keep you forever."

"Not if I keep you first." That response makes zero sense, but Dex laughs anyway, and I feel that laughter everywhere we touch, including in his enormous cock.

"I'm going to love this baby I'm giving you. I'll take care

of you both, love you both so well, you'll never want for anything. I already love you and this baby so much." He looks right into my eyes and it's a good thing I'm on my back and tied up, because I'm a mess. A sloppy, destroyed, custard pie of a girl. To go with the cream pie he'll make me.

"Dex, I can't wait. Please. Fill me up." Some lust-drunk part of my brain must be saying these things, because it wouldn't be me, who was a virgin only a week ago, right?

"I will."

He's jolting me, and despite how brutal Dex is being, pleasure mounts.

"Dex, I think I'm going..." Then I can't speak, because Dex alters the angle of my leg, and my mind goes static-y.

"I can't get enough of you," he rumbles. "You're mine, and I can't live without you, little one. You're the centre of my soul. You've made me alive again."

I break. The pleasure that had been threatening like a summer day with sparks in the air, shatters into cracks of lightning and thunderous rain.

"Fucck..." Above me, Dex's face is scrunched, intense and feral as I tighten around his very solid length. "That's it, little one. Milk it out of me. Take it."

I'm sobbing. I've never felt anything like this.

He thrusts once, twice, and then embeds himself deep in me.

His roar is triumph and ecstasy and pain, and I feel him pump wet heat into me, seemingly under my ribcage, right by my heart. He shudders. His grey eyes are soft but intense as he doesn't hide from me. He lets me see how shaken he is, how our love drowns us both. His face is savage and contorted and his breathing harsh, his mouth open as his shout fades to a growl.

I swear I can feel his seed as he fills me with hot fluid.

"Take your fill," he groans as he collapses, his bulk pressing me down. "It's all for you, I'm yours."

There's spurt after spurt as he's wracked by his orgasm so hard it looks almost painful. But he never stops looking into my eyes, and this is the moment I've been waiting for.

Dex. Me. Our love and making our baby.

"I needed this," I confess rawly. "I needed you to come inside me."

"I know, little one, I know. Me too."

So we can have a baby, of course, but I craved the feeling of him breaking apart like that. It was nothing less than magic. His weight on top of me and the way he's given me his seed, filling me with it, is intimacy I never thought I'd feel.

He murmurs something about not wanting to squash me, and I protest as he rolls onto his side and takes me with him. It's so good. I'm drugged with how wonderful it is to love Dex and be loved by him in return.

It's minutes or hours later when I come to. Dex has looped his arm under my thighs and is dragging me up.

"What?"

"Lift your hips," he directs roughly.

"Why?" I'm baffled.

"Because you're not going to allow any of my seed to leak out, are you?"

He slants one eyebrow, and my heart skips.

"No." I shake my head. "Keep it in." I guess gravity will do its thing eventually, but the idea of remaining full of Dex's come heats me from the inside out in a way that I can't explain.

Kneeling between my legs, Dex sighs contentedly, and my grumpy, serious boss smiles when he glances up at me. "Fuck, little one. I've wanted to do this since we met."

"Really?" I'm too content for this to be real.

His expression is pure, satisfied evil as he settles down.

"That's right." He gives me a long, leisurely lick all the way up my slit then sucks his lower lip, as though savouring my taste. "I wanted to feel you come. I wanted to taste you, and you're so fucking sweet. And most of all, I wanted to taste you and me together while I keep you wet and ready for me until I breed you again."

"Dex…" I breathe his name. How am I this lucky?

He pushes my thighs wider. "Let me see all of you."

I'm so exposed, but instead of feeling vulnerable, I'm excited and happy and bubbling with more arousal than I could have believed possible.

He licks me with the kind of dedication most people only give to things that benefit themselves. He's single-minded, like I'm his whole world. And I'm powerless to do anything but what he wants of me. He might be doing this for me, but he's my god.

I come screaming his name, as he doesn't let up for a second, but somehow knows exactly where I'm too sensitive and licks me through every earth-shattering pulse. He leaves me a mess. I'm flat on my back, twitching, pleasure bouncing off each cell in my body.

"Dex," I murmur weakly. He's destroyed me.

"Little one." And then he's over me again. His cock nudges at my entrance. "Do you want extra seed?"

"Yes." Was I tired? Pah.

The push of his renewed erection into my gaped, soaking pussy reignites me. I'm vibrating with need once more.

"That's it." He kisses my lips tenderly as he slides all the way in. "I love the feel of my warm come inside you. I might keep you like this forever."

It's so good, so intimate and I'm so entirely loved. I wrap my arms and legs around my husband and urge him on.

"Please, husband. Breed me."

"I will." The next stroke is firmer. "If you tell me again."

"Breed me," I pant.

"Mm." He almost purrs with contentment. "That too. But the other thing." Reaching up, he combs his fingers into my hair and then fists it, drawing a gasp from me. "The other words, wife."

"I love you. I love you, I love you." It's a chant as he increases his pace.

"Fuck, I love you too," he growls, as he holds me. "So much, little one."

Then he slams into me, and we're both lost in each other.

EPILOGUE
DEX

8 Years later

There is a moment dreaded by every mafia boss who loves his children.

In the open doorway to Sophia and my bedroom, seven-year-old Raina stands with a confused furrow in her brow and her hands on her hips. I glance between my eldest child and my wife, pleading with both to not make me do this.

"Daddy?"

"Yes, I heard you, Raina." I try for the strict tone I used to use with my men who were messing about and now use for bedtimes that get raucous. Admittedly, I am usually to blame for starting the play at bedtime. I can't resist another half an hour with my kids. All five of them. "Close the door as you leave. We can talk about this later."

Or never.

Sophia snorts and continues unbuttoning my shirt.

"What happened?" Raina asks in a small voice. That

nearly breaks me. Even Sophia's clever fingers pause. "Are you hurt, Daddy?"

Most parents worry about their children asking about how babies are made, walking in on them having sex, insulting their uncle, or falling off their bicycles.

Most mafia bosses worry about their territory, power, and lives.

But the top concern these days for the London Mafia Syndicate kingpins—including me—is how to explain to our respective children that sometimes people have to die, and occasionally that process gets blood on our clothes.

"It's okay, baby girl, I'm not hurt," I say gently. I still have my *little one* and my *good girl*—Sophia—but I love that I now have three perfect *baby girls* and two *little buddies*. The five children Sophia has gifted me with to spoil and love.

"But Daddy, there's blood." Raina has switched with the remarkable efficiency of a child from utter distress like a puppy left alone all night, to a fully grown bloodhound tracking a scent. "Whose blood is it, Daddy?"

"Canary Wharf is right," she says quietly enough that Raina can't hear as she takes my wrist and flicks off the cufflinks. Her wry smile adds, "I told you so". "You should change your shirts before you come home."

I look down at my wife, and she looks up at me.

"For the younger kids, anyway," she adds. "Maybe it's time to talk with the biggest baby about the family business?"

Her undressing me when I've caught someone I'm after is a tradition begun after I killed the Essex Cartel man who shot at her—us—after the night that everything changed. I still have the scar, but it's the memory of that night when I got revenge which really lingers.

Sophia helped me out of blood-stained clothes, then as a rare allowance, I allowed her to wash me in the shower. To cleanse me of all my sins.

Inevitably, her naked in the shower with me leads to her being pushed up against the wall, me getting to my knees and licking her out until she screams. And then sex, all wet and slippery, and soaking everything in the bedroom with water... and other liquids.

Very satisfying all round. I was looking forward to it.

I sigh. Catching up my wife's hands, I kiss them. The shower sex will have to wait.

"Can you get me a clean shirt?" I murmur to Sophia, and she nods.

"Okay, baby girl," I say to Raina. "Come in and close the door. Pop yourself onto the sofa and you can ask your questions."

None of us will have any peace until my daughter knows more. She's determined and brave, just like her mother. And she is seven. She can understand a little.

I hope.

When I'm in fresh clothes, I take my place next to my daughter on the cushions. This is our cosy private relaxing space, away from the hubbub of the rest of the house with the nanny and our younger kids. Sophia and I sit on either side of Raina, and we explain, in simple terms, about how some bad men want to hurt people, and sometimes we have to stop them.

I leave out the intricacies of how we brought down the worst parts of the Essex Cartel, and some of the details that are pure protective rage. My daughter doesn't need to know that when I returned home to her and Sophia after dealing with the Essex Cartel assassin, it was like I'd been swimming in red.

I was very angry with the man who nearly shot Sophie.

"Sometimes we have to stop people from doing cruel things," I finish. What we found in the container echoes through my head, and for a second, I imagine any of my family in that situation, and my fists clench. "It's like we discussed about animals, remember? They have to die."

She frowns, digging deep lines in her forehead.

"What is it?" I ask, with some trepidation. I hope my daughter hasn't developed a strict moral code that I can't—

"Should we eat them?"

"What?! No!"

So much for strict moral code. I appear to have raised a savage little cannibal.

"But we ate the lambs from that farm we went to," she argues with apparent reasonableness. "And you said that it was normal. Part of the circle of life, you said."

"I did *not* say to eat humans." I am very certain about that.

"You *just* said that this was like animals." She pouts.

God help me.

Out of the corner of my eye I can see Sophia covering her mouth to prevent herself from snort-laughing.

Damnit, this never happens in Sophia's romcoms. I've read a lot of them now, and I'm positive there isn't one—even the dark ones—where a murderous kingpin has to talk his child out of cannibalism. I suppose I was due some bad luck when I've been blessed with my wife, my five children —so far—and having destroyed the Essex Cartel, but really.

"It is in some ways, but not others," I say.

"So that rule applies only to animals?" Raina asks seriously. "The one about eating them or it's a waste."

"Yes." I think we're back on solid territory. This is fine. No inappropriate consumption—

"What about dogs?"

"No." Zero positive thoughts that I'm on the right track until this conversation is entirely over. I just tempted fate. "We don't eat dogs. We don't eat anything that eats other animals."

"What about insects?"

"They're okay." I hold my breath, waiting for her to bring up another scenario. Goats, perhaps. Or pigs. Did I tell the kids about pigs eating bodies? Please, please no. And I really hope I didn't mention vegetarianism.

"It's confusing," she tells me with absolute confidence of a child who knows her father will also fix things and always explain it all.

"Yes." It's hard to admit there's no simple explanation. I want to be a parent who protects and makes the world perfect for my kids, but even I can't manage that.

Raina nods seriously.

"Daddy," she says in that voice that announces she has a question, and she's not sure I'll like it.

"Yes, baby girl."

"Can we go to the park?"

Oh thank god.

A grin spreads across my face. "Yes, we can go to the park."

I look out over Streatham Common less often now, but when I do, it's more enjoyable. I used to feel alone and isolated when I saw families. But now I have Sophia, and the kids. I have everything I want.

"With everyone?" Raina checks.

"Yes, the whole family."

Above Raina's head I catch Sophia's eye and our gazes lock. Her expression is full of relief that this conversation went well, and my heart expands.

Sometimes I just cannot stop looking at my wife. This is one of those moments. She's perfect, glowing, and sweet. The opposite of me, and yet she's mine.

"We'll all go to the park," Sophia agrees. But the way she bites her lip tells me she hasn't forgotten what we were about to do before our eldest baby interrupted.

Tonight, I silently promise her.

EXTENDED EPILOGUE
DEX

8 years later that evening

"Dex." Sophia emerges from the bathroom wrapped in a towel as I'm sitting on the edge of our king-sized bed and removing my watch.

It's been a good afternoon, after the small hiccup of having to explain to our daughter about not the birds and the bees, but the bats and the bones.

My wife is holding a small plastic stick. My eyes go wide.

And now, I realise I might have spoken too soon. Birds and the bees might be in order soon too, as excitement unfurls in my chest.

"Sophia," I echo her severely. "Have you got something you need to tell me?"

"Maybe..." She sashays across the room towards me, a naughty smile playing over her lips. "Look for yourself."

"You've only been off birth control about a month," I say wondering.

"That's all it takes with us." Her smile is happy as she shows me the result panel.

And there on the test is the unmistakable sign.

"You're pregnant." I raise my gaze to my wife, and I know my heart is in my eyes. Also, my cock is getting hard.

"Ready for your sixth baby, Daddy?" she teases.

"I'm glad you don't waste everything I give you." I stroke her flat belly over the towel. She's lined with stretch marks from when it's been swollen with my babies, and that only makes me hotter for her. She's covered in signs of my ownership. That she's had my children. Been bred by me.

Fuck, she's so gorgeous.

"Such a good girl," I rumble. "Getting pregnant for me. I'm always impressed. You value your husband's sperm, don't you?"

"I never waste it when I could get pregnant," she replies, and the other part of that sentence hangs in the air.

I stand abruptly. There's something we've done five times before at exactly this moment, and yes. If she's going to suggest it, I'll take advantage.

"Get on your knees," I bark, and she's obeyed, discarding her towel instantly, before I've even opened my flies to withdraw my aching cock.

"Yes, Mr Streatham." Her voice is all breathy with arousal, and she licks her lips.

"Does my little come slut want this?" I grip my cock and give it a couple of pumps as I look down at her. "Do you want it down your throat?"

"Yes."

That eagerness undoes me. I thought I'd never have her because she's too good for me, too sweet and innocent and lovely. Even now, years on, I cannot believe my luck.

I cup her cheek and admire Sophia's pink lips.

"You want me to fuck your mouth, my pregnant whore of a wife?" I murmur, and although the words are gruff and harsh, my touch is gentle. For now.

"Please." She blinks up at me, and opens her lips invitingly.

Then I angle my cock and slide it right into her mouth.

"Fuuuccck. My god, little one. That is..." I still don't have words for how good it feels when Sophia accepts me enthusiastically into her body. Her mouth and pussy, especially. She's hot and wet and eager, so eager. "Yes, do that," I manage to choke out as she presses onto me, the head right at the back of her mouth.

Though I tell myself I hold her hair to control her, tug it a bit to make her moan and get her slick between her legs, it's not. It's holding onto my sanity by a thread.

She opens her throat, and her hand finds my thigh, digging in her nails to tell me to use her. My pretty girl has practised time and time again until she can deepthroat me, and I grunt as my eyes cross at the first stroke.

I give in, as I always do, and thrust. The pleasure notches up instantly and hell, but I can't make this last tonight. After I was so controlled during the first week of our marriage, Sophia consistently made it her mission to find every little thing that made me lose it.

Her eyes water but she doesn't shut them or look away as I fuck her mouth.

"You're being such a good girl for me," I murmur, shoving deeper and it feels like heaven.

She's hypnotic like this, and I've admitted to her that when she lets me in, that's what I can't resist. So this conscious opening is the oddest mutual weakness as we both give in to each other. I use her because she wants me to, and I'm her slave because I'd do anything to be even a millimetre closer to her.

I guess that's love.

And the way she's growing our child in that soft tummy is her greatest acceptance of me of all.

My balls pull up, and need tingles at the base of my spine. I won't last much longer like this, ramming into her wet, willing throat.

Grabbing her hand, I place it on the base of my cock then pull back and slow down. A pinch of disapproval makes furrows between Sophia's eyes, and I rub them away.

"Not like that today, wife."

"Mmm." Her hum is entirely eloquent, and makes me even harder, which is no doubt her intention.

"You want my come, don't you?"

She makes a wordless whine of assent, and sucks me harder, her hand working the inches not in her mouth. The slip of my cock into her, and the rhythm of her fingers is driving me crazy.

"You want to taste it?" I know that's what she wants. After we were so careful about me coming at first, it's still a luxury to cover her with it, or let her swallow. "Or do you want me to cover your face? Get it in your hair, and all over your tits?"

She squirms and her cheeks are going red as I say these filthy things to her.

"I love it when you blush. Reminds me of that day in the office, all those years ago. You were a come slut, even then, weren't you?"

Tilting her head back, I pull from her again, and take my cock in my hand. She gazes up at me as I give it one, then a second stroke, the point of no return arriving.

"Close your eyes, darling," I growl, and then it hits me.

I come, barely able to focus as the hot white liquid hits Sophia's face, her mouth open. The pleasure crashes over me as my seed spurts out. I slide my fist over my length, drawing out my orgasm as my come drips onto my wife's tits.

"Fuck, little one," I groan. "Every time I think you can't be any sexier, you outdo yourself."

My brat opens her patterned eyes and smirks as she licks her lips and swallows like I'm the best thing she's ever tasted.

"Get up here." My voice is hoarse.

She rises on shaking legs, and I wrap my arms around her and lift her so we're level. "I love you so, so much," I say, the intensity of her blow job making me savage. "You'll always be my precious, treasured wife. And my slut."

Then I kiss her, and I feel her nodding as I don't allow her breath to say anything. The taste of my come is a tang that shivers taboo down my spine. She clings to my shoulders, and I fall back onto our bed, her on top of me. I squeeze her tight and kiss her deeply. Despite her weight on me, my chest expands with love and happiness.

I love you, I tell her with my kiss. *I love everything about you.*

We're a sopping mess. Her cream is leaking out from between her legs and onto my thigh. My come is all over her face and mine. Her saliva is dripping from my cock.

But none of that matters. We'll go and shower, then get dirty all over again, this time with my head between her legs until she's coming with a scream.

My girl is pregnant again. We're increasing our family. We're spreading our love.

And best of all, we're together. Nothing has meaning without Sophia.

She's my world.

THANKS

Thank you for reading, I hope you enjoyed it.

Want to read a little more Happily Ever After? Click to get exclusive epilogues and free stories! or head to EvieRoseAuthor.com

If you have a moment, I'd really appreciate a review wherever you like to talk about books. Reviews, however brief, help readers find stories they'll love.

Love to get the news first? Follow me on your favored social media platform - I love to chat to readers and you get all the latest gossip.

If the newsletter is too much like commitment, I recommend following me on BookBub, where you'll just get new release notifications and deals.

- amazon.com/author/evierose
- bookbub.com/authors/evie-rose
- instagram.com/evieroseauthor
- tiktok.com/@EvieRoseAuthor

INSTALOVE BY EVIE ROSE

Stalker Kingpins

Spoiled by my Stalker

From the moment we lock eyes, I'm his lucky girl… But there's a price to pay

Kingpin's Baby

I beg the Kingpin for help… And he offers marriage.

Owned by her Enemy

I didn't expect the ruthless new kingpin—an older man, gorgeous and hard—to extract such a price for a ceasefire: an arranged marriage.

His Public Claim

My first time is sold to my brother's best friend

Pregnant by the Mafia Boss

Baby Proposal

My boss walked in on me buying "magic juice" online… And now he's demanding to be my baby's daddy!

Groom Gamble

I accidentally gave my hot boss my list of requirements for a perfect husband: tall, gray eyes, nice smile, big d*ck. High sperm count.

Grumpy Bosses

Older Hotter Grumpier

My billionaire boss catches me reading when I should be working. And the punishment...?

Tall, Dark, and Grumpy

When my boss comes to fetch me from a bar, I'm expecting him to go nuts that I'm drunk and described my fake boyfriend just like him. But he demands marriage...

Silver Fox Grump

He was my teacher, and my first off-limits crush. Now he's my stalker, and my boss.

London Mafia Bosses

Captured by the Mafia Boss

I might be an innocent runaway, but I'm at my friend's funeral to avenge her murder by the mafia boss: King.

Taken by the Kingpin

Tall, dark, older and dangerous, I shouldn't want him.

Stolen by the Mafia King

I didn't know he has been watching me all this time.

I had a plan to escape. Everything is going perfectly at my wedding rehearsal dinner until *he* turns up.

Caught by the Kingpin

The kingpin growls a warning that I shouldn't try his patience by attempting to escape.

There's no way I'm staying as his little prisoner.

Claimed by the Mobster

I'm in love with my ex-boyfriend's dad: a dangerous and powerful mafia boss twice my age.

Snatched by the Bratva

I have an excruciating crush on this man who comes into the coffee shop. Every day. He's older, gorgeous, perfectly dressed. He has a Russian accent and silver eyes.

Kidnapped by the Mafia Boss

I locked myself in the bathroom when my date pulled out a knife. Then a tall dark rescuer crashed through the door… and kidnapped me.

Held by the Bratva

"Who hurt you?"

Before I know it, my gorgeous neighbour has scooped me up into his arms and taken me to his penthouse. And he won't let me go.

Seized by the Mafia King

I'm kidnapped from my wedding

Filthy Scottish Kingpins

Forbidden Appeal

He's older and rich, and my teenage crush re-surfaces as I beg the former kingpin to help me escape a mafia arranged marriage. He stares at me like I'm a temptress he wants to banish, but we're snowed in at his Scottish castle.

Captive Desires

I was sent to kill him, but he's captured me, and I'm at his mercy. He says he'll let me go if I beg him to take his...

Eager Housewife

Her best friend's dad is advertising for a free use convenient housewife, and she's the perfect applicant.

Printed in Dunstable, United Kingdom